Write It Right:

Exercises to Unlock the Writer in Everyone

* * *

Workbook #5

Units 9, 10: Conflict/Tension; Subplot

By
Susan Tuttle

Susan Tuttle

Write It Right:
Exercises to Unlock the Writer In Everyone
Unit 9: Conflict/Tension
Unit 10: Subplot

Susan's website and blog: www.SusanTuttleWrites.com
Email Susan at: aim2write@yahoo.com
Follow Susan on Twitter: @stuttleauthor, Facebook and LinkedIn

Cover design by: Aaron Kondziela (www.aaronkondziela.com)

A WriterWithin Publication

ISBN-10: 1941465080
ISBN-13: 978-1-941465-08-0

Write It Right:

Exercises to Unlock the Writer in Everyone

Workbook #5:

Conflict/Tension, Subplot

Dedication

The first unit contained herein, the ninth skill of the series, *Conflict/ Tension,* is dedicated to Anne Peterson, an amazing writer, who took me under her wing, introduced me to SLO NightWriters, and encouraged a very timid writer to trust herself and her talent. I wouldn't be here without you, Anne.

Subplot, the second unit in this Workbook, and the tenth skill in the *Write It Right* series, is dedicated to another "Anne"—Anna Unkovich, a truly fabulous writer herself. She took up where Anne Peterson left off and kicks my behind to keep me on the straight and narrow. I'm anxiously awaiting her first book, a story that grew from short story to novel length as she worked through our class. See, Anna, I told you one day you'd need to learn about subplots!

Contents

Before You Begin

SUCCESSFUL STORYTELLING LIES IN being able to tell the story you need to tell in the way readers need to hear it. When we do that, we create stories that readers cannot put down. There are many steps along the way. The first three, *Character*, *Setting* and *Story*, are contained in Workbook #1. The next most important element, *Point of View*, is presented in Workbook #2. Workbook #3 covers the next two most important skills: *Plot* and *Dialogue*. Workbook #4 explores *Scenes* and *Style/Voice*. This volume, Workbook #5, discusses *Conflict/Tension* and *Subplot*.

Unlike other books on writing, this volume is designed as a workbook to help you hone your writing skills and find your unique voice. Within these pages, you will find **18 exercises** designed **for writers of all levels** that will show you how to craft enthralling tales readers will love. You will discover strategies to help you create and ramp up tension and conflict that will keep readers on the edge of their seats. And you'll learn how to craft enticing subplots that reflect and deepen your main plot, while adding drama, spice and intrigue to your stories.

In the few pages that follow is all the front matter that most people simply skip. If you haven't started with any of the other Workbooks, please read what follows, especially the *Foreword* and *The Value of*

Timed Writing. They contain invaluable information you will need to get the most out of these lessons and exercises. And even if you have read it already, please at least skim over *The Value of Timed Writing* once again, to reacquaint yourself with the "rules" of each lesson.

And of course, don't skip the book list. Go out and purchase them all. They are invaluable treasures for your writing library.

Foreword

WRITING IS MY LIFE. I have a thousand stories knocking on the inside of my head, seeking the freedom of paper. I also love to learn, especially about writing and ways to improve my range and skills. But I'm not very disciplined when it comes to how-to books. If it's not a mystery or suspense novel, I lose interest quickly, even if the subject matter is fascinating.

I found that, for me, the best way to learn something is to teach it to someone else. So, four-plus years ago, I decided to start a group where I could teach what I wanted to learn about writing techniques. If nothing else, it would force me to read those "how to write" books I've been collecting.

I formed the *"What If?* Writing Group" (which has now been renamed as the *"Write It Right"* Writing Group) through SLO NightWriters on the Central Coast of California. I began with a group of six writers of various writing skills and genres. We met once a week for two hours to explore in depth a specific aspect of fiction writing. I worried at first that, given the weekly commitment, the group would gradually peter out. But not only did they keep showing up, they started arranging appointments and planning trips around the lessons so they wouldn't miss any!

As the year began winding down, I was sure this group would go on its literary way, and I wondered how to attract a new group of students. But when the year was up only one person left the group, due to health problems. Everyone else wanted to repeat the course. We picked up three new members and started again from the beginning, not sure if the original six students would get anything much from the repetition. To the contrary, we discovered the exercises worked just as well as the first time around—and in some instances, even better. It seems that, no matter where you are in your writing journey, or how many times you do these exercises, they continue to work. Every time.

These students are now getting published on a regular basis, and winning awards in writing contests. In fact, three of us won first place awards in different categories at the Central Coast Writers Conference in September of 2011. One even came home with three prizes in the competition! For me, this was proof positive that the **Write It Right** exercises had a hand in unlocking the talent of every member of the group. That's why I added an afternoon class and 8 more students.

The writing successes of both of the *"What If? Writing Groups"* made me wish I could reach more writers with the materials we'd used. But even if I taught classes all day, every day, I could reach only a limited number of writers—and all of them local. I wanted more than that. I wanted to reach all writers, everywhere.

To that end, I decided to collect all the lessons into a series of 12 little instruction workbooks, a full program called **Write It Right: Exercises to Unlock the Writer in Everyone**. This workbook is the fifth Compendium of the series. Volumes 1-4 are also available in print format from Amazon.com. At this writing (August 2015), I'm hard at work on the sixth volume, ***Brilliant Beginnings and Extraordinary Endings***, which hopefully will be out by October or November, 2015. And there's a seventh volume knocking at the back of my mind, strategies for self-editing and a primer on the digitals and technicals all writers need to know these days. So, keep an eye out for Volumes #6 and #7!

Introduction to Workbook #5

READERS NEED A REASON to keep turning pages. That reason is intricately interwoven with the story question: Will he? Will she? Will they? Writers need to enhance each situation to make the reader wonder if the protagonist will succeed, or if the antagonist will be the victor. This enhancement is done through the use of conflict, also known as tension. **Conflict/Tension** (also referred to as suspense and defined as strain, pressure or friction, not mystery) is the main element that puts readers on the edge of their seats, biting their nails, unable to put the book down.

While conflict is easy to find in many stories—indeed, mystery, suspense and thrillers are built around dangerous situations filled with tension—**all stories must have some kind of conflict/tension**. Even literary and experimental tales must have tension built into them, or they will become tedious and boring and readers will shut the book partway through, if they bother to pick it up in the first place. Carefully crafted tension that builds throughout the story until the final point of confrontation, where the main story questions is answered—Will he? Will she? Will they?—is what makes a story worth reading.

Subplots do much more than simply enlarge your story so there are more pages to read. In fact, if that's all they do, then they have no place in your tale. To be viable, subplots must either act as a mirror to the main plot, deepen the theme and/or enhance the growth of the characters throughout the story.

Let's say your main character is trying to solve a crime, the theft of her grandmother's necklace. You know you need some quiet times, breaks from the suspense and tension for readers to breathe, so you decide to write a parallel plot of the main character preparing for a quilt show. This might be a wonderful look into the character's normal, everyday life. And it might be well written and engaging. But if it doesn't somehow tie into the main plot—the search for the necklace thief—it will leave readers wondering just what the story was about: the quilt show, or the theft. The subplot about the quilt show needs to be **connected** to the main plot by reflecting it, deepening it, or helping the main character solve the mystery in some way.

That is where this Workbook comes in. The exercises that follow will give you the strategies you need to understand conflict and tension and how they work to keep readers turning pages. And you'll learn how to create subplots that enhance your main plots and make readers say, "Wow!" The nine lessons on conflict/tension will help you understand just what tension is and the vital role it plays in making your stories come alive for readers. The nine Subplot exercises will give you the techniques you need to interweave intriguing subplots through your stories, one that will enhance and strengthen the main plots.

It won't happen overnight. It takes practice. But the more you work with *Write It Right: Conflict/Tension and Subplot*, the better you will become at recognizing even the most subtle deviations in your narrative.

It doesn't matter what level you are: beginner, intermediate or advanced. These exercises cross those boundaries and address where you are now in your writing career—and get you to where you want to be.

These are not time-intensive sessions. You only need to **dedicate approximately 30-45 minutes** to most of the eighteen activities (a few may take longer). Feel free to move at your own pace—one or two exercises a week or a month—but if you choose a fast-track pace, do give yourself enough time assimilate each lesson. It's best to have a couple of days between each exercise. (The original *"What If?* Writing Group"— now renamed "The *Write It Right* Writing Group"—which has used these lessons for over four years as of this writing, does one or two exercises per session, with a week between sessions.)

All you need is a timer and something to write with—pen and paper or computer and keyboard, whichever is most comfortable for you. For maximum results, you might want to pick up a copy of some of the books I've used to formulate these lessons, and which I will reference throughout most of the course. It's not necessary, though it does make understanding some of the concepts easier.

You can use this volume as a workbook, writing on the pages (though you will need extra paper to finish most of the exercises) as you work through the lessons. But it is best to use separate sheets of paper, or work digitally in a word processing program, so that when you return to the lessons at a later time you won't be distracted by previous answers to the lesson questions.

Always remember, this is **an ongoing process**. Writing is a dynamic art and life is a journey through which you are always growing and learning. Over time your writing will expand and deepen to reflect these life experiences. When you finish this volume (or any of the exercises in the other volumes), you can repeat each of the exercises again, just as we do in "The *Write It Right* Writing Group"—which at this writing is nearing the end of its fourth year of repetition, with mostly the same students. You'll find that the second, and even third and fourth (or more), time around your writing will reach even deeper layers and take you to greater heights. It will be stronger, more compelling and more exciting.

It's a fantastic journey. Plunge into the exercises in *Write It Right: Conflict/Tension and Subplot* and experience what it means to really understand the narrative potentials available to you.

The Value of Timed Writing

MOST OF THE EXERCISES in this course are timed. You have a specified amount of time to complete each one, usually 15 to 30 minutes. An hour at the most, broken into increments. That's it. Period.

Why timed writing? There are two major benefits to timed-limited sessions. As **Natalie Goldman** shows in **Writing Down The Bones**, timed writing exercises force you to keep writing. You have a specific goal and only a short time in which to accomplish it. You have to step out of your way, turn off your inner editor—who is constantly saying you've used the wrong word, no one will believe that plot, your characters aren't "real" enough, etc.—and simply write. From your heart, from your subconscious instincts, from the place where your stories live. It's authentic writing that's scraped to the bone of emotion. It's compelling and readers will want more.

The second benefit is that you learn to **trust yourself and your writing process.** When we learn to put our conscious mind on hold and just let the words flow, amazing things happen. Stories emerge that we never knew were there. Connections get made that our conscious minds would never have considered. Best of all, our authentic voice emerges, announcing in clear, ringing tones, "This is who I am as a writer. This is what I need to say." Timed writing exercises will introduce you to yourself.

Timed exercises allow you to step away from your editor self and into your writer self because you don't have time to think. You have to just keep writing, no matter what comes out. It may be hard at first not to go back and correct that word, rethink that action, direct the flow, etc. It takes time to learn to trust your instincts. When you find yourself wanting to go back, don't. *Write* about wanting to go back until you return to the natural flow of the exercise. You can always cut out the extraneous parts later. That's what editing is for.

Timed Writing Format "Rules"

Read the lesson, make sure you understand what to do, then set your timer and write until it dings. Don't stop to think, don't edit as you go, just keep your pen moving or your fingers typing on the keyboard. If you can't think of anything at first, write about not being able to think of anything and just see what happens. Repeat for the next lesson. And the next, and the next...

Also, be aware that my use of the terms "character," "person," "people," "he" and "she" are meant to indicate the protagonists, antagonists and other characters in your stories, whether they be humans, animals or otherworldly creatures. Make whatever adjustments you need to make to each exercise, so that it fits your specific genre and character choice.

Note: An asterisk at the end of an exercise denotes that there is an example of that exercise from my own writing at the end of the section.

Recommended Book List

THESE BOOKS, AMONG OTHERS, have been instrumental in the formation of these lessons. For those in Unit #9, I reference the pertinent page or pages to read for the appropriate lesson as I did for the skill units in Volumes 1 to 4. Although you don't need these books to complete the lessons, the information they contain is invaluable. It will add to your knowledge and skills and enhance your learning throughout this series. And they will form a solid foundation for your writer's reference library.

I am listing the copyright year for each of the volume I used in my research. If you want to read the suggested pages noted in each lesson, you will have the correct volume in which to find them. How-to books are often updated with new examples and insights. If you obtain a volume published after the dates listed below, you will still get the same fantastic writing information. But because things will have shifted around in newer editions, you might have trouble finding the proper references for each lesson unless you use a volume with the same publication date as those listed on the next page. (Note: *Unit #10, Subplots*, does not use these references.)

Write Away by Elizabeth George (2004)

What If? Writing Exercise for Writers by Anne Bernays and Pamela Painter (1990)

On Writing by Stephen King (2000)

Characters & Viewpoint by Orson Scott Card (1988)

How to Write a Damn Good Novel by James N. Frey (1987)

The Novel Writer's Toolkit by Bob Mayer (2003)

Finding Your Writer's Voice: A Guide to Creative Fiction by Thaisa Frank and Dorothy Wall (1994)

The 38 Most Common Fiction Writing Mistakes by Jack M. Bickham (1992)

Make A Scene: Crafting a Powerful Story One Scene at a Time by Jordan E. Rosenfeld (2008)

And every writer's library should contain the following reference volumes:

*The biggest dictionary you can afford (check used bookstores for bargains). There's no substitute for a good, print dictionary

*Roget's Thesaurus

*Sisson's Synonms (if you can find it)

*The Elements of Style (Strunk and White)

*Barron's Essentials of English

Unit 8: Conflict/Tension

"The suspense of a novel is not only in the reader, but in the novelist, who is intensely curious about what will happen to the hero."

~Mary McCarthy

SUSPENSE IS ESSENTIAL TO the success of every novel. Without some kind of suspense, the reader has no reason to continue reading. Pages turn only because readers want to know what will happen. And they want to know because there is the possibility that the "right" thing might not happen—at least until the end of the book.

We're not talking about suspense in the sense of the mystery and thriller genres. The kind of suspense I mean, that all books need, can be defined as a sense of tightness, a pressure, a wonderment and feeling of curiosity that must be satisfied.

Every novel, no matter what it is about, must have suspense built into it, or readers will not bother reading it. Suspense, which in this sense means conflict/tension, is what compels readers to keep turning pages to see what will happen.

For instance: Will Phil ever be able to please his boss? Will Kathy and Brad marry? Will Marcie and Doug succeed in conceiving a child? Will the Wilsons ever hear from their runaway son? Will Mason's conscience force him to confess his adultery? Will Frannie win a place in the ballet corps? Will Sarah find true love when she studies abroad in France? Will the new puppy ever find his place among the older dogs in the household?

Not a traditional mystery, suspense or thriller story among the above, and yet each one needs its own underlying feeling of suspense, of tension, of "what will happen?" on every page in order for the tale to be compelling enough for readers to read to the end.

Think of your story as a series of blind corridors that cant off in all directions. You can't see around corners, you just have to pick a direction and turn. Anything can happen when you step into that new corridor. There could be a monster waiting to devour you. There could be a trap door that opens and drops you into a dungeon. There could be snakes or rats or spiderwebs. Or a pit filled with water. Or an oracle who will give you a clue. Or a clear corridor leading you to the next blind corner.

That's the point: You just don't know. And not knowing, *but needing to know*, produces pressure, anxiety, tightness. That nail-biting feeling of "What will happen?" when you step around into the unknown, is the tension that needs to underscore every scene in your book. The reader, who stands at that blind corner with your characters, wondering, worrying, anxious to see, will have to step around it with them (i.e., turn the page), in order to find the answer to the question: What's waiting up ahead?

If you want a less intense example, consider your chapters as wrapped birthday presents awaiting you on a table. Each is a different shape and size, wrapped in a variety of colorful papers. And they are all for you, every one of them. Don't you feel a sense of tension rising just at the thought of opening them? What do they contain? Is the big one better than the small one? Does the red paper cover a more coveted present than the green paper? Is the heavier one worth more than the lighter one?

Suspense. Tension. Curiosity. That's what drives readers forward, compels them to unwrap each scene, each chapter, like wonderful, exciting, mysterious birthday gifts.

Now it's your turn to flip the page and discover what the next nine exercises can teach you about how to box and sheath your chapters in the gift wrap of conflict/tension/suspense.

Unit 9, Conflict/Tension: Contents

Lesson #1: Intention in Characters

TENSION COMES FROM NOT knowing, but needing to know. And for that to happen your story needs two things: a character readers can bond with, and something vital that is at stake.

In other words, give readers a character they care about, a character who is determined to do or get something, and you have readers who cannot wait to find out if it will happen or not. Give readers a second character who is determined to do or get something that will interfere with the first character's intention, and you have a story that cannot be put down.

The key is to **know your main characters' intentions** before you begin to write the story, and to state those intentions when the characters are first introduced to readers. A character's intention can be multiple as those listed by Richard in his opening siloloquy in Shakespeare's *Richard III*, where he clearly says he intends to pit his brothers against each other and plant a false prophesy that will imprison one of them, because he intends the throne to be his. Or the intention can be singular, as in *Pride and Prejudice*, when Mrs. Bennet says, "What a fine thing for our girls!... You must know that I am thinking of his marrying one of them."

Think of the books you have read. Weren't there some that left you wondering for a while—some of them for quite a while—what the point of the story was? What did the main character want? How did the antagonist oppose that desire? Or, put another way: What was at stake and was it dire enough to hold your interest?

Chances are, you didn't finish reading those books. You put them down and found something else that grabbed you right away and wouldn't let go. If you did continue reading, it was probably tedious or even boring to plow through that long, rambling opening until you finally realized what the story was really about. And when you did discover it, was it urgent enough to make you *need* to read on, to find out if the main character would prevail in the end? Maybe. Maybe not.

Think of the stories you have written. Where in the manuscript did the intention of your protagonist become clear? Where did the intention of the antagonist come clear? It should be **when each character is first introduced to the reader**—or very close to that point. If not, you will need to go back and rewrite those all-important introduction scenes.

Now look at the intentions of your two main characters. **Are their intentions truly in opposition?** If not, your story will lack that sense of tension that keeps readers turning pages. Without two forces opposing each other, with consequences that promise to be life changing for both of them (either positively or negatively), there isn't enough to make readers *have* to continue on to see what will happen. The tension that keeps pages turning will dissipate and the story will feel flat and boring.

Always remember, readers want to read about characters being tested; characters who have to overcome great odds to achieve their hearts' desires. I had a writer friend once who couldn't grasp that concept. She hated conflict of any kind, and so her stories lacked conflict between her characters. Everything was always easy. Whatever a character wanted, he tried once and achieved his end, with no one opposing him or trying to stop him. She wasn't a bad writer and her story concepts were interesting, but she left out the one thing that would make readers want to continue reading—tension. No one had to wonder, "Will he?" or "Will she?" because the outcome was never in doubt in the first place. Whenever I read her stories, I found myself wondering when something of interest would begin. And it never did.

Knowing your main characters' intentions, and stating them clearly when each character is introduced, will set up that all-important "need to know" in the reader. And it will help keep you focused as you write, because you will have those opposing intentions firmly in mind. Character A wants something. Character B stops her. Character A regroups and finds a way around Character B. Character B strikes out and once again stops Character A. And on and on, with the battles between them (physical, mental, emotional and/or verbal) growing in intensity, until one finally prevails.

Now you have a story that readers can't put down.

READ: *Write Away* (George, 2004) Page 43-44.

Exercise #1: Intention in Characters*

(Purpose of Exercise: to find tension in a character's intention)

CREATE A CHARACTER WHO will be the protagonist of a story. Write a short bio of this character, detailing his/her strengths and weaknesses, the things that will make the reader care for him/her.

Now, give this character an intention. It can be a single intention, as Mrs. Bennett's intention of having Mr. Bingley marry one of her daughters in *Pride and Prejudice,* or a multiple, interwoven intention as is Richard III's opening intention in Shakespeare's play.

Set your timer for **15 MINUTES** for this part of the exercise.

Part II: When you have finished with the intention of the protagonist, do the same for the antagonist of a story: a short bio and his/her intention(s) which, of course, must conflict with those of the protagonist. The intention(s) of the protagonist should have already given you a glimmer of a story idea, so make sure the antagonist's intentions weave into and work against those intentions.

Set your timer for **15 MINUTES** and write about the antagonist and his/her intention, starting now.

Lesson #2: How Many Ways?

AS WE DISCOVERED IN the last exercise, a sense of suspense or tension can come from the opposing intentions of the main characters. But that is not the only place tension can be found in stories. Using a number of ways to increase tension will make your stories even more suspenseful and, therefore, more enticing to readers.

Creating an **internal conflict** within a character is a great way to add tension. Take a moral character and put him in a situation where he needs to choose between his desire to do what is right and a need to break his own moral code, and you will have readers on the edge of their seats. Will Raymond remain true to his marriage vows, or will he succumb to the wiles of his first, long-lost, true love who has resurfaced in his life? Will Dr. Ellery succumb to the desire to damage the person whose drunken drivings ended his daughter's life, or will he stay true to his Hippocratic oath? The key is to make this kind of conflict the indecision and ambivalence that are common to everyone. Let the character suffer the kinds of feelings we all suffer from time to time: doubt, fear, guilt, worry. Then, as these characters struggle with the imbalance inside them, readers will avidly flip pages to discover the outcome.

There are many other ways to increase tension in your work. Pit human against nature by making a weather phenomenon or natural disaster the antagonist in the story. Judicious selection of details can make nature appear as a formidable opponent who seems to thwart the human protagonist at every turn. *The Perfect Storm* uses the weather as a formidable opponent; in *Into Thin Air*, Mount Everest is the nemesis against which the humans must strive.

The animal world offers many ways to insert tension, as humans and animals each clash in order to achieve their opposing desires. This doesn't mean animals have to be anthropomorphized. Consider *Jaws*, where the shark is merely being the perfect aggressor of his species. Even in *Cujo*, the dog is not imbued with human characteristics, he is merely the pawn of a deadly disease that makes him a fearsome danger to those around him. And both novels are not put-downable.

Rivals from the spiritual dimension can make perfect opponents for the human characters in your stories. Read through such tales as The *Exorcist, The Amityville Horror* and *The Shining* to see how man struggling against the supernatural can make tension almost unbearable. The same can be said for alternate realities and aliens, whether on this planet or somewhere in the far reaches of the galaxy. The Star Wars series uses alien concepts as the perfect foil for human needs and desires.

Remember that **conflict is merely a form of collision**. It doesn't always have to be the men in the white hats against the men in the black hats. That concept limits you and your stories. Learn to find the "collision" in a wide variety of places, the places where man's will comes into conflict with an immovable person, animal, situation or object. When the character is put into conflict, when he is faced with a dilemma and forced to make a decision, forced to act, he becomes real for readers. This kind of dramatic conflict equals anticipation for the reader, and the reader who anticipates the outcome will continue reading to the end.

Anticipation, excitement, interest and compassion; these all come from the tension we craft into our stories.

READ: Write Away (George, 2004) Page 60-62; end of page 62 to break in page 63.

Exercise #2: How Many Ways?*

(Purpose of Exercise: To explore the places where tension comes from)

FOR THIS EXERCISE, TRY to list at least **6 different types of tension** and show how they could be used to ramp up the suspense in a story. Give your imagination free reign here to fully explore the different ways you can insert tension into a story to keep readers turning pages. Consider the types of stories you don't normally write as you list the different types of tension.

Set your timer for **20 MINUTES** and keep listing the different avenues where tension/suspense can come from in a story until you have at least 6 different types and how they can add tension. If you have time left on the timer when you are done, continue listing more types of suspense/tension until the timer dings.

Lesson #3: The Crucible

WHAT IS A CRUCIBLE? Moses Malevinsky, in *The Science of Playwriting*, says that a crucible is "the plot, or the furnace" in which the drama is "boiled, baked, stewed or hibernated." It is "one of the most important elements of [a drama's] organic structure."

Why? What makes a crucible so crucial to a story? And how do we find the crucible in each of our stories?

A crucible is the situation, or container if you will, that **holds the characters together** as the action unfolds. The moment we reveal the conflict between our characters, readers will begin to ask questions like, "If the boss is so bad, why doesn't Phil just quit and get a job somewhere else?" or "Why don't Marcie and Doug just adopt?" or "Why can't Mason forgive himself and not put the burden on his wife?" If we don't give compelling reasons why the character has to deal with the situation **as it is**, the story will lack believability. The characters *must* be bonded to the situation, unable to break free, compelled to continue dealing with whatever happens.

The crucible provides that essential bond. Characters who are bonded together won't, as Lajos Egri points out, "make a truce in the middle and call it quits."

You create a crucible by making the character's motivation to stay in conflict **greater** than the motivation to run away from it. Put your characters in a crucible where the protagonist and antagonist, for their separate reasons, are committed to continuing the conflict until a final resolution is reached—the boss is finally pleased, Marcie gets pregnant or they agree to adopt, Mason chooses to forgive himself and save his wife the agony of his infidelity, or whatever.

Remember, without conflict there is no drama, and without a crucible there is no conflict. If the bond is missing, the characters are free to walk away at any time. That is why crafting a crucible to fit your story is essential.

Consider these examples of crucibles from two of my books. (Spoiler alert: these descriptions give away some of the plot in the stories, in case you haven't read them yet.)

From my book, *Sins of the Past*. Sabrina is being pursued by the man who killed her husband. Mitch, an FBI agent, arrives to protect her and catch the killer, a hit man won't get paid until he gets the information he needs from Sabrina. They are trapped together in a deserted inn during a hurricane. The storm is their crucible.

Here's another from *Proof of Identity*. Danae Holloway has to prove she is not a killer even though her fingerprints are on the knife. Jenna Strogan needs to revenge herself on her enemies before she dies of a brain tumor. The psychic bond that links them is their crucible.

READ: *How To Write A Damn Good Novel* (Frey, 1987), Page 31-34, stop at end of first paragraph

*Exercise #3: The Crucible**

(Purpose of Exercise: To explore the crucible situation)

PUT THE TWO CHARACTERS you created for exercise #1 into a crucible situation (a place, time and circumstance from which they cannot walk away). Write out what the situation is, detailing **why** they cannot get out of it without seeing it through. Remember, not being able to get out of the situation without seeing it through is what makes it a crucible.

Now, brainstorm the conflicts that might arise as they deal with the crucible situation, and list them. Take **15 minutes** to do this part.

Now take what you think is the **most important**, or serious, conflict, and tell how that will affect the characters and solve the crucible situation. You're not writing the scene, just listing how the chosen conflict will affect the situation and characters as it answers the story question.

Now study the list and start numbering them, beginning with the least urgent or serious conflict and working toward the most important, or most serious, making each conflict build upon the previous one.

When you finish arranging the conflicts from least urgent to most urgent, answer the following questions. How much more tension/ suspense does having multiple, increasing conflicts have on your story? How much more interesting do you think it will be for the reader to have more than one conflict adding tension to the story?

Set your timer for **20 MINUTES** for this part and start writing.

Lesson #4: Crucible Situations

THERE ARE MANY WAYS to craft crucibles. They are not simply physical situations, though those may be easiest to see and understand at first. Put opposing characters in a runaway train car, an inn in a blizzard, a boat in the ocean during a tropical storm, and you have an easily recognizable crucible.

But crucible bonds can be crafted from many other types of situations. Inner conflicts can make a crucible: A man has a job he hates and where he is belittled by his boss on a daily basis. But he cannot leave the job because he has nine kids at home and could never find another job that paid enough to support his family. His need is his crucible.

Marcie and Doug want to conceive a child, but nothing seems to be working. Marcie wants to adopt someone else's child; Doug cannot bring himself to even consider taking in a child who is not his own. Their philosophical disconnect is their crucible.

When crafting a crucible for your characters to strive in, keep asking, "What is stopping them from walking away? What makes this so important they will keep on toward their goal?" If you can't find a compelling answer to those questions, you don't yet have a crucible.

When crafting your crucible, consider philosophy, psychology, theology, science, emotions, the paranormal, mental and physical ailments and limitations, geography, weather, plants, animals—anything that can you can turn into a situation from which your characters cannot walk away, a situation in which they must struggle and strive to come out the other side.

Here are some examples of bonding from some well-known works:

One Flew Over the Cuckoo's Nest: McMurphy is incarcerated in a mental hospital; he cannot leave. All Big Nurse cares about in life is to control her ward. The mental hospital is their crucible.

The Old Man and the Sea: The old man needs the fish on the line to prove his manhood. The fish can't get free from the barbed hook in its mouth. The death struggle is their crucible.

The Godfather: Nick Corleone must stop his enemies or his family will be smashed. His enemies need to take the power for their families. Duty to their respective families is their crucible.

Madame Bovary: Emma is married to a man she detests, but divorce is not possible in her day. The marriage is their crucible.

Lolita: Humbert Humbert love Lolita. She is a child with nowhere else to go. His love and her dependency is their crucible.

As you can see, a crucible can be comprised of many things, not just a physical place the characters cannot leave. It can be a sense of duty, of failure, or of love; it can be a partnership of some kind, a need to stay together or a need to pull apart when staying together or pulling apart is impossible. It is the *bonding* of the opposing characters that forms the crucible, and once the crucible is established readers will have to read to the end to see how the main character manages to release him- or herself from the situation.

Craft an inescapable crucible and give your characters inner conflicts on top of it, and you will have a story that can't be put down.

READ: *How To Write A Damn Good Novel* (Frey, 1987) Page 36-39

Exercise #4: Crucible Situations*

(Purpose of Exercise: To explore crucible situations)

CREATE AT LEAST FIVE crucible situations that could be used to create tension in stories. Give a short description of the situation, the two (or more) characters involved in the scene, and the reason (or reasons) why they are caught in the crucible (in other words, what makes it a Crucible). Consider whether you would have a hero and a villain (good vs evil), or a protagonist and an antagonist (two good people—or two evil people—at opposition) in each situation. Tell why you think this is best for the story.

Set your timer for 25 MINUTES and begin describing your crucible situations. This gives you 5 minutes per situation. Start now.

Lesson #5: The Horns of a Dilemma

ONE OF THE BEST ways to ramp up suspense or tension in your story is to give your characters an inner conflict that adds to the difficulty of dealing with the crucible situation. Whenever duty collides with fear, love clashes with guilt, ambition wars with conscience, etc., you have what is called a moral dilemma. In other words, the character is impaled on the horns of a dilemma.

This moral dilemma serves two purposes: to ramp up the tension within the crucible, thereby guaranteeing the reader will continue reading on; and to connect the reader with the character on a very personal level. He or she becomes truly memorable to the reader.

Inner conflicts make the characters real because we all struggle with such conflicts ourselves at various points in our lives. Just as they do to us, inner conflicts will make our characters hesitate. Like real people they will waffle, and waver, and wallow in indecision. They will have doubts, feel guilt, remorse, fear, misgivings, and second thoughts. Readers will cheer them on, hoping they will choose the right outcome, the moral outcome, just as we hope we ourselves would do the same.

This connection creates empathy for the character, and that can be extremely powerful. And not just for your protagonist. Imagine an antagonist who has no inner conflict about any of his actions. He would appear one-dimensional to readers, almost unbelievable. But give him an inner conflict where he struggles against feelings of guilt over what he has or wants to do, and he becomes a real human with needs and desires and hopes and fears. Readers now understand why this character is who and what he is, the factors in his life that have shaped him and haunt him. They begin to hope there is some kind of redemption for this character, that somehow, in the midst of the chaos and evil, he will change and grow in a more positive direction.

How much more effective and engrossing is a story where there is hope not only for the protagonist, but also for the antagonist. And no reader will be able to resist reading to the end to see what will happen to both characters.

In creating inner conflict, you don't need to have earth-shattering issues at stake. It only needs to *seem* that way **in the mind of the character**. For example, one man may torture himself over wanting to kiss a woman other than his wife, while another married man blithely sleeps with every available woman without a lick of conscience. There is more inherent drama in the story of a man who regrets just thinking about another woman if that thought means he loses his sense of integrity and honor, than in the story of a man who has no regrets about sleeping around indiscriminately.

The trick is to make sure the character is reluctant to do or not do something for *very powerful reasons*. It must be a true crisis of the character's conscience, of his/her moral fiber. There must be as compelling a reason for the character to have or to do something as there is for him not to have it or not to do it. You know your character is impaled on the horns of a true dilemma when the forces pulling him in opposite directions are **equally powerful**.

When you create your characters, both protagonists and antagonists, look for the dilemmas that will help build so much tension that readers will not be able to put the story down until it is finished.

READ: *How To Write A Damn Good Novel* (Frey, 1987) Page 36-39, "Inner conflict and the necessity thereof"

Exercise #5: The Horns of a Dilemma*

(Purpose of Exercise: To use inner conflict to create tension)

CHOOSE ONE OF THE crucible situations from Exercise #4 and give **each** of the main characters (the protagonist and the antagonist) an inner conflict. As much as inner conflict is vital to making the reader empathize with your main character (and thus keep reading), it is equally important in the antagonist, so that character doesn't end up being a cardboard cutout. No one is all good or all evil. The easiest way to portray the human failings with which the reader can identify is to give the character an inner conflict.

What inner conflicts will you give these two characters? Start with the protagonist and try to brainstorm at least three or four conflicts that could work for the story. Is your first idea really the best? Often it is not the most clever, or the one with the most workable twist. That's why it's important to try to think past your first idea of inner conflict to the deeper ones, the ones that might catch the reader's interest even more. Pick the one that most appeals to you.

Once you have a list for the protagonist, then make a list of three or four conflicts that the antagonist could have. Which one will most work against the inner conflict of the protagonist? Or will cause the antagonist the most difficulty in opposing the protagonist?

Give yourself **20 MINUTES** to finish this exercise. Set your timer and begin writing.

Lesson #6: Character Development as Key to Conflict

WHERE DOES ONE FIND the inner conflicts that are key to both tension and connecting readers to the characters? The best place is in the background of the characters, in what has happened to them before the story even starts. How the characters grew up, who and what influenced them, the events that befell them, the people who accepted and rejected them, the types of philosophy, psychology and religion they are exposed to, all go into making them who they are. From all of that comes their belief system, their needs, wants and desires, and what they believes they are capable of—and not capable of. Humans are shaped by what happens to them in childhood; a person's entire life is influenced by those long-ago events. That is why a detailed biography of each of your main characters is so vital.

Most importantly, when you tap into those beliefs that grow out of early life, you tap into feelings that are universal to most people. The circumstances may be unique to each character, but what they feel—fear, doubt, worthlessness, anxiety, shame, hope, love, sympathy, etc.—are emotions we all feel at times. Once readers recognize the emotions your characters are struggling to overcome or master, they bond with the characters. They care about what happens to them. And they cannot put the book down without reading to the end to see what will happen to them.

The character arc—how the character grows and develops throughout the story—will of necessity pull out those elements of the character's background that are essential to creating a deep sense of tension that will not let readers go. For instance, suppose you have a character who has always been told by his parents that he will never amount to anything. He struggles with feelings of worthlessness as he attempts to make a success of his life. Since we have all felt like that at times, as readers we can empathize with this character. We bond with him. Tension rises as we wait to see if he will be a success, or if he will end up fulfilling what he believes is his parents' expectation for him: to be a failure.

Now put him on the horns of a dilemma: The woman he secretly loves faces unwarranted disgrace if he does his job properly, if he indeed succeeds. If he doesn't, he is the one who faces dismissal and disgrace, thereby fulfilling his parents' expectation. His success means her downfall. His dilemma: He must choose between protecting the woman he loves and proving his parents were right—he will never succeed—and doing his job properly, thereby proving his parents were wrong about him—he can succeed. The connection between this character and readers strengthens almost to the breaking point as the story progresses. Readers will be on the edge of their seats as they turn pages, waiting to see the outcome of this character's struggle.

Who we are at any one point in time is the end product of all that has happened to us in the past. The same holds true for our characters. They do not appear out of a vacuum and then disappear back into it when the story ends. They had a whole life before the beginning of the story, a life that shaped their personality, their thoughts, their beliefs, their philosophy of life. And when the story ends, they will go back to living the rest of that life, "off stage," as it were.

It is in the events of a character's past that the seeds of inner conflict can be found. Mine those events with care and you will find just the exact dilemma for your character that will keep readers turning pages until the end.

READ: Write Away (George, 2004), page 167-173

*Exercise #6: Character Development as Key to Conflict**

(Purpose of Exercise: To find conflict in character development)

USE A CHARACTER FROM a story you are working on, one you created for the last exercise, or create a new character for this exercise. Tell who the character is as the story begins, and how you visualize the character will change as the story develops.

What challenges do you foresee the character facing? How do these challenges affect his/her development? How does the character's background, his/her upbringing, affect how he/she faces these challenges? Is the tension you visualize steady, jumping or rising?

Look for and note places where or how tension can be added: at crucial plot points; put a character in physical, psychological or emotional risk; use physical, emotional or verbal abuse; insert a momentous discovery; create time limitations; devise a MacGuffin*; foreshadow future events, etc.

Set your timer for **15 MINUTES** and begin writing.

*See Page 30 for a description of a MacGuffin if you're unfamiliar with the term

Lesson #7: Opening Scene Tension

THE MOST IMPORTANT PART of your story is the way it opens. If you don't hook readers at the very beginning, chances are you won't keep them reading much further than the first few pages.

Most people, while browsing for their next story, will open books and read the first page—sometimes only the first few sentences. At best you have about 5 to 10 seconds to intrigue readers so deeply they will be compelled to purchase the book in order to find out the rest of the story. If you don't, they will put your book down and pick up someone else's.

Five to ten seconds. The fate of your story rests on those all-important snippets of time. You can have the best, most exciting, most entrancing story of all time, but if the opening does not grab readers, it will never be read.

When crafting the opening of your story, keep in mind **The Rule of Firsts: Stick To The What**. For the *first* sentence, *first* paragraph, *first* page, *first* chapter, concentrate on the "what" of the story. Leave the "why" for later. In these four "firsts" (sentence, paragraph, page, chapter) you need to write with capturing your audience foremost in your mind. Once the reader is hooked and can't put the story down, you will have more leeway in the details and structure of the scenes, and inn revealing backstory. Once the reader is hooked you can begin to include the "why." But readers must first be completely and thoroughly hooked on the "what" before you venture into the "why."

One of the biggest mistakes writers make in the first few pages of a story is to put in the backstory; that is, those things that happened before the story itself begins, and that constitute not *what* is happening but *why* is it happening. However, **the opening is the worst place for backstory**. By its very nature, backstory is narrative that slows down the action, interrupts the forward momentum of the story, and inundates the reader with details that have little or no meaning to them at this point.

For example, after work hours Joe is embezzling funds from his uncle's bank to pay off gambling debts. He gambles because his father once took him to a casino when he was eight and Joe's slot machine paid out a big jackpot. It was the only time his father was proud of him, and Joe longs to make his father proud of him again. Putting all that backstory in while Joe is hiding from the security guard and the cops because he inadvertently tripped the alarm will slow down the action and drain the tension. Plus, readers don't know Joe at all at this point, so they won't care about *why* he is embezzling funds, they only care about *what is happening*, whether or not he will be caught.

We will delve more deeply into the 8 ways of crafting the first sentence in Workbook #6's Unit eleven, *Brilliant Beginnings*. Right now we will work with the opening scene of the story, all four of the "Firsts."

Start with an opening that grabs at the reader's emotions, curiosity or attention. Give them ongoing action that will intrigue and fascinate them. Insert an element of danger—physical or emotional or even spiritual—drop clues to future events, tantalize with bare facts, and let the reader know what is at stake, what the antagonist stands to lose. And if possible, end the chapter with a cliff hanger, to keep those pages turning.

Here's an example of a first chapter, with the elements noted in brackets: For my in-progress YA fantasy, *Destany's Daughter*, I start with an opening sentence that tugs at heartstrings: *The moment Meleia saw him at the top of the garden she knew her mother had died.* [Emotional grabber] From Meleia's reaction, we learn only that her mother had warned her about this person [emotional danger], and that she knows who he is—though the text does not enlighten the reader at this point. The horseman chases and captures Meleia and takes her through a portal that knocks her unconscious [physical danger]. When she awakens, she finds herself in a barren room guarded by an invisible force field. Her captor arrives and through their fiery interaction we learn he is her uncle, that he is responsible for her mother's death [tantalizing facts], that Meleia is important to him for some reason and that something called the Imperium is involved [clues to future events]. The uncle threatens Meleia with violence, which erupts when she tries to escape [more physical danger]. The chapter ends with Meleia shut alone in the room once again, beaten and bloody, desperately trying to hold onto her consciousness [her freedom and her life are at stake].

Readers are left with many questions: How did Meleia's mother die? Did the uncle actually kill her? Why is Meleia important? What does the uncle want from her? What is the Imperium? How far is the uncle willing to go to get what he needs from his niece? Will Meleia break and give him what he wants? How will she get out of her prison room? By using the Rule of Firsts and sticking to what was happening instead of why, I was able to craft an exciting beginning that makes readers want to discover the answers by reading on.

The secret to crafting a mesmerizing opening is to constantly ask, "*What* does the reader need to know at this point to understand *what* is happening?" Notice I did not say *why* it is happening, but only *what* is happening. That is because **the why often will slow down the action**. The why also answers the questions that readers formulate as they read: Why is Marcie going out with this guy? Why is this watch so important to Curt? Why doesn't Grace want Mel to know she's been in the museum before? If readers already know the why, they have no reason to read on.

Concentrating on what is happening sets up the why questions in readers's minds, but does not supply answers. They have to keep reading to learn the answers. And using the Rule of Firsts to craft your opening helps you avoid dumping a load of backstory into the narrative in a place where it doesn't belong.

Readers need to get to know the characters a bit first so the backstory will have meaning for them. If the backstory is inserted too early, when they don't know the character, they haven't had enough time to bond with the character to care about all those whys. And if the backstory is inserted anywhere in one huge chunk—another big mistake often made by writers—then all the questions will be answered and the overall tension of the piece will suffer.

When it comes to backstory, always ask, "What part of the backstory does the reader have to know **right now**, and what can be **reserved for later**?" Spreading the backstory throughout the main story helps keep readers turning pages to discover the answers to their questions.

There are a number of elements you can include in your opening scene/chapter to hook readers. Among them: a crucial plot point; the character(s) at risk, either physically, psychologically or emotionally; a chase; violence of some kind, either physical or verbal; a momentous discovery; a critical time limitation; a MacGuffin*; items/people/actions that foreshadow future events; tiny snippets of backstory **that set up questions** in readers' minds (that is the only time to use backstory in your opening).

By making sure to concentrate on *what* is happening rather than why, and by choosing your details carefully, you can craft an opening that will have readers clamoring to read on.

*FYI, a MacGuffin is a plot device in the form of a goal, desired object, person, place, or even a driving force of some kind, that the protagonist (or antagonist) pursues with little or no narrative explanation. The specific nature of a MacGuffin typically is not important to the overall plot of the story.

The most well-known MacGuffin is arguably the priceless statue in the movie, *The Maltese Falcon*. Everyone is after it, but why—and exactly what the statue is—is never fully revealed. Other examples of MacGuffins are: the meaning of rosebud in *Citizen Kane*; the briefcase in *Pulp Fiction*; Krieger Waves in the *Star Trek: The Next Generation* episode "A Matter of Perspective"; the Hellmouth in *Buffy the Vampire Slayer* (a topographical MacGuffin); the television set in the novel *54* (by Wu Ming); and the container in *Spook Country* (by William Gibson).

Exercise #7: Opening Scene Tension*
(Purpose of Exercise: To use tension as a way to lure readers into a story from the first sentence)

Stating with the paraphrase (below) of the beginning of the novel *A Certain Smile* by Fracoise Sagan, write a short scene that will draw the reader to one of the characters and form a bond with him or her. Think of this as the opening of a story or a novel. The aim here is to **hook the reader** on the character so that the reader is compelled to find out what fate has in store for that character.

While writing the scene, try to infuse it with the beginnings of tension/conflict in one or two of the following areas (this is a short scene so two will be more than enough) : a crucial plot point; put the character at risk (physical, psychological or emotional); a chase; violence of some kind (physical or verbal); a momentous discovery is made; time is limited; a MacGuffin appears. If possible, pepper the scene with items/people/ actions that could foreshadow future events. Underline these, so you don't forget to put them into play later.

Final Query: If you were to finish this story, do you think you would you keep the first line the same, or would you change it? Why?

Paraphrase: We had spent the afternoon in a cafe, a winter afternoon just like any other.

Give yourself **20 MINUTES** to write this scene. Set your timer and begin writing now.

Lesson #8: Handling Fear, Suspense and Terror

EVEN IF YOU DON'T write mystery, suspense or thrillers, there will probably come a time when you will need to write a scene that is filled with the more traditional suspense, fear and terror that characterizes the mystery genre. Of course, all your stories need to have strong elements of suspense (as in a feeling of anticipation), but being able to master working with the strong emotions of actual fear and terror will make your writing rise to the next level. And it will keep readers clamoring for more because it will feel completely real to them when it is called for in your story.

You need to be able to handle all strong emotions, not only traditional fear, suspense and terror, but also passion, hatred, anger, depression, envy, shame, despair, arrogance, pride and love, among others. Taking the time to practice bringing these emotions to the fore now, before you need to tap into them for a work-in-progress, will make your job writing your story that much easier. You may never write a mystery or thriller, but understanding how to use the elements of those genres will add depth and richness to the tales you do write.

The key is to **mine your own life** for instances when you felt the same emotions your characters are dealing with. We may not want to admit that our dislike of that person was actually hatred—hatred strong enough to prompt us to want to harm that person, even though we did not act on the impulse—or that we were so terrified being alone at night at that "ideal" cabin in the woods that we dissolved into tears and hid under the blankets (or the bed), but when we allow ourselves to remember what we felt—how our bodies reacted, what thoughts went through our minds, what impulses shot through us—we can paint a realistic picture of what our characters are going through.

It's this feeling of realism we are after. When it's real for our characters, it will be real for our readers. And it can't be truly real for our characters until it's real for us, the writers. Take me as an example. I write mysteries, about murder and murderers. I'm in and out of some really creepy heads when I write. I certainly have no idea what it feels like to kill, or even physically injure, another human being (or animal, for that matter). In fact, I'm so squeamish on the subject I can't even watch the evening news before I go to bed or I'll have nightmares all night.

But I do know how it feels to be angry enough to *want* to kill or harm someone. I'm not proud of the feeling, and I don't often admit it, but I am, after all, human. And I know how it feels to be so scared I turn into a gibbering idiot and head for the bedcovers. But emotions are part of the human condition. They are neither right nor wrong, they simply are, a fact of the life we live. It's what we do with our emotions that can impact our life—and the lives of others—positively or negatively. My choice is to use what I feel to create stories that readers will enjoy and hopefully learn something positive from. And so I do what I need to do, no matter how hard. I go into my own feelings, revisit what is sometimes not at all pleasant (and sometimes downright nasty), then twist that reality to fit my characters and plots. Even if it means a sleepless night or two.

And you just may find you need a time in your non-mystery story when your character is terrified. Perhaps she's home alone in a new house, hearing weird noises she can't identify. And she can't remember if she locked the door. Or closed the windows downstairs. Or your hero was held up by road constrution and his one true love has just departed town on the train, or a plane, thinking he didn't care enough to stop her. Or your character said something vile and hateful that caused someone problems, and now is so ashamed he or she can't go on living. Or a mother has just lost her only child to illness or accident. Or the limousine is t-boned on the way to the wedding reception and the groom is killed. Or a teen suffers so much guilt over lying and cheating he/she contemplates suicide.

Not a traditional mystery or thriller in the bunch. But you still have to handle a deeply emotional, gut wrenching scene with a sense of reality and aplomb. Take the time to periodically play with isolated scenes that evoke these kinds of emotions, so you get used to tapping into your own life experience as you craft your story. When you can tap into the more painful parts of your humanity, it's easier to write believable scenes. Ane only by tapping into your own emotions can you step fully into the shoes of characters totally unlike yourself and render their stories faithfully to your readers. Who will then clamor for more.

READ: What If? (Bernays & Painter, 1990), Page 118

Exercise #8: Handling Fear, Suspense and Terror*

(Purpose of Exercise: To learn to handle the really creepy stuff)

YOU'RE AT HOME ALONE. It's late at night and you are not expecting anyone to arrive home until the morning. The doors to the house or apartment are locked. You decide to take a shower and because you are alone, you do not lock the bathroom door. During your shower, you hear a strange noise in a room beyond the bathroom.

Write what happens. You can use either first person or third person to tell the story. Don't spend any time getting into the shower; you're already there when the scene starts. Concentrate on creating as much rising suspense as you can. As you write, be sure to add details of setting and character that make the scene full and rich.

Set your timer for **20 MINUTES** and start writing.

Lesson #9: Analyzing Ideas for True Conflict

AS WE HAVE DISCUSSED, all stories need conflict. It's the clash, the opposition, the colliding forces, that pull readers on through the action to the end. Without conflict, without opposition, there's no urgency and no need to discover the answer to the story question.

But sometimes, in the excitement of burgeoning ideas, writers can be blind to what constitutes true conflict. It's easy to mistake bad luck, fate or mere adversity with the kind of conflict that sets up the struggle that makes readers turn pages. Always keep in mind that when there isn't an opposing force against which to struggle, there's no real way your hero can persevere and overcome.

The kinds of problems that at first may seem viable—fate, bad luck, adversity—are blind. They simply occur out of the blue. There is no human—or otherworldly—agency behind them plotting and planning to make your hero's life even more difficult or impossible. They simply happen, regardless of anything else that is going on in the character's life. The character can struggle *through* these events, but cannot struggle *against* them and come out the winner. The character can merely persevere until the circumstances either go away or shift to someone else.

Remember, while conflict implies violence of some kind, not all conflict is defined as a physical confrontation. There are verbal conflicts, philosophical conflicts, emotional conflicts, mental conflicts, theological conflicts, scientific conflicts, etc. All a conflict is, in essence, is a fight of some kind, where the hero has to act to achieve a goal and change his/her world. Using fate, bad luck or adversity might feel at first like a good strategy, but these are things that cannot be changed. They simply exist. They happen without rhyme or reason, as it were, and must simply be suffered through instead of acted upon. And if there is no true fight, no true achievement of a goal, no change in the hero's world—for the positive or the negative, depending on the story—then there is no true story there at all.

To give you an example, say you have a story about a couple who have a fight about his affair with another woman just before he leaves for a business trip to a dangerous area overseas. The wife, afraid she will lose him, races to intercept her partner before he boards the plane, so they can get things right between them. But she catches every red light between her home and the airport, and thus misses the plane.

Or you have a character who has been trying for years to break into show business. He finally has a second call-back where he is only one of two actors up for a juicy role in a new television series. But on the way out of the house he trips on a crack in the sidewalk and breaks a leg, losing out on the role.

These kinds of events are unfortunate. They are the kind of bad luck, or fate, or adversity we all suffer through at times in our lives. And at first they seem like a good idea for your story. Yes, they will make your character's life more difficult for a while. But they are not true instances of conflict. There is nothing that can be done about lights that turn red on whatever arbitrary timetable has been set, or a foot catching on the cracks in the sidewalk. They are not things that can be fought against, only persevered through until the circumstances ease up. Which they will do on their own, with no action on the part of the characters.

But, if the wife's car has been tampered with *by the mistress* so it will stop running and she will miss the plane, now you have someone against whom the wife can struggle. Or if *the rival* for that juicy role affixed a trip wire across the walk in order to injure our actor hero, then there's a human agency against whom he can battle. The events didn't just happen for no reason. They were caused by someone with an opposing goal. And that opposing goal sets up the fight to come. Now you have true conflict and a story worth writing, and reading.

When you sit and brainstorm your ideas of how to make life even more difficult for your hero, how to make that ultimate goal ever harder to reach, be sure to analyze your ideas to make sure you are not relying on events that are triggered by fate, adversity or mere bad luck. If they are, figure out how to twist them to include that all-essential human (or inhuman) behind-the-scenes agent against whom your hero can battle. With a human—or inhuman or otherworldly, as the case may be—agent behind the difficulties your hero encounters, you'll have a fight to the finish that readers won't be able to put down.

READ: *The 38 Most Common Fiction Writing Mistakes* (Bickham, 1992) Page 25-26

Exercise #9: Analyzing Ideas for True Conflict

(Purpose of Exercise: To discover which story ideas contain true conflict)

Go back to Exercise #4 in **Workbook#1, Unit 3: Story** (p. 93-96) and look at your ideas. (If you have not yet done the exercises in Volume 3, see the exercise below. Give yourself **15 minutes** to finish that exercise. When you are finished, then begin this exercise).

Now analyze your answers to this exercise. Are all the story statements true instances of conflict, or are some just adversity, fate or bad luck? If they are, how can you change them to reflect true conflict?

Take 15 minutes to finish this analysis of your story ideas.

From Workbook #1, Story: Exercise #4: Multiple Story Possibilities

CRAFT A STORY STATEMENT for a new story. Ex: "What If... a repressed housewife feels her husband doesn't love her and she gets a job as a pole dancer?" Continuing asking "What If...?" Questions to find scene and plot possibilities. Ex: What if she gets in debt with the owner of the place? What if the interest is structured so that she can never pay it off but she doesn't realize it? What if the owner makes her do private lap dances to pay off her debt? What if the owner wants her to do full nude dancing? What it if rains every time she leaves for work and is late? Continue brainstorming possibilities for **15 minutes**, then do the analysis exercise above.

Examples From My Class Writing

Please bear in mind that all the following examples were written during timed writing sessions in my classes and have not been edited or rewritten.

Lesson #1: Intention in Characters

Character: Jordonna Edora

Jordonna is in her early 30s and has just been released from a prison sentence of 6 years for cat burglary. She was raised by her father, an international jewel thief, after being kidnapped from her mother at three years old. She has two brothers who have followed their father into the family business, and one who ran away at age 16 and hasn't been heard from since. Jordonnas's father abused her emotionally, made her completely dependent on his approval, and she has spent her life trying to win that approval, which he always dangled in front of her but never fully gave her. During their last heist together, he abandoned her when she inadvertently triggered the alarm, even though he could have gotten her away without being caught. She expected that he would somehow rescue her from the law, but nothing happened except that she went to prison. There she realized how trapped she'd been by him, and began to see the way she'd been manipulated to do his bidding. And that she was merely a means to an end for him. He'd never really loved her, or wanted her love.

Released from prison, she has no money, no job and nowhere to go. She is struggling with not returning to the only way she knows to obtain money. She wants to build a normal life, but is finding that her ex-con status allows her little freedom to change her ways. She has a soft heart and is easily wounded, but has learned not to cry and to pick herself up and start over whenever she needs to. She is trying to figure out how to exact revenge on her father and not get caught.

Her intent: To rescue her 10-yr-old half-sister, Lolly, who was also kidnapped by her father and is being taught to take Jordonna's place in the family business, and to raise her as her own, because their mother is incompetent. And to destroy her father and not get caught.

Character: Kettering Savage

Kettering is an only child who was indulged by his grandparents who raised him after his parents were killed in a small-plane crash. They both died within a year of each other when he was a senior in high school. He is independently wealthy, but hates to be idle. He has tried all sorts of jobs, but finds he hates routine, regulations and working with others. He wants to do things his own way. He has opened a private detective agency and specializes in finding missing persons. He has only two friends, who he lets get only so close; everyone else he holds at arm's length with an aloof attitude and a tendency to irony. He is terrified to get too close to people because they just leave in the end. He has been hired by Lolly's mother, Virginia, to find her and bring her home, and has fallen in love with Virginia.

His Intent: to find Lolly Mason and bring her home to her mother, Virginia, and to put the father in jail where he belongs.

Lesson #2: How Many Ways?

1) From within an individual:

Jordonna struggles with knowing only one way to gain money—by thievery—and wanting to go 'straight' and obey the law, even though no one will give her a job or a place to live.

2) Between two people:

Jessie wants to settle down and start a family; Michael, who loves Jessie to distraction, doesn't know who he is or what he wants from life. The last thing he wants is a family.

3) Between man and desert:

Jake's Jeep breaks down in the middle of the Sahara desert and he must find his way to civilization.

4) Between Cop and Psychic:

The hard-nosed, it-ain't-real-if-I-can't-see-it detective refuses the help of a psychic who can see images in the murder's mind, which won't go away until she helps the cops catch him.

5) Between humans and aliens:

Corbin and Rhen battle intelligent alien machines that reduce all matter to dust.

6) Between Ideals

Celira wants everything to stay the same, while Loric wants to continue on his evolutionary path.

Lesson #3: The Crucible

Crucible: A fierce storm rages, shaking the earth. Meleia's uncle, Laskin, pursues both Emril and Meleia, and Meleia's twin Tane, through the storm and into the cavern where the Cask of Immutability is hidden. An earthquake seals the cavern entrance and they are caught in the cavern. No one else knows where they are, which way they ran when the storm hit and Laskin discovered them. Now they are sealed in the cave with the Cask calling to them, and Laskin there to kill them and steal the Cask once it is opened.

1. Laskin stays hidden, following Emril and the twins who aren't sure he was caught in the cavern with them.

2. Meleia doesn't want to find the Cask until she is sure Tane is no longer in their uncle's thrall.

3. Tane doesn't trust Meleia not to seize power for herself.

4. Emril and Tane are physically antagonistic toward each other.

5. The twins are drawn irresistibly toward the place where the Cask is secreted.

6. The kids hear Laskin's footsteps echo in the cavern and realize he is following them.

7. Rocks tumble from the ceiling and walls, sealing off their escape as they proceed further into the cavern.

8. Meleia tries to turn Tane from the right way, but he can hear the Cask calling to him.

9. Emril and Tane fight over who will protect Meleia.

10. Laskin captures Meleia and uses her to force Tane to find the Cask.

11. Emril pretends to sprain an ankle and tries to use the ensuing confusion to attack Laskin to free Meleia, which doesn't work.

12. Laskin exchanges Meleia for Emril to force the twins to work together to open the Cask.

13. The twins open the Cask of Immutability and empower the Ring of Reality.

14. Laskin offers to exchange Emril for the Ring and to let them all go.

Lesson #4: Crucible Situations

1. Crucible = A group of people on a train in the mountains for a sightseeing tour. A landslide on a steep downgrade separates the engine and first two cars, and screws up the mechanics on the engine, so the brakes fail:

Protagonist: Detective Sergeant of police department on vacation with his wife. Motivation = to stop the train and save the passengers' lives, especially his pregnant wife's.

Protagonist: Disgraced Navy SEAL who has been looking for a way to redeem himself. Motivation = to stop the train and become a celebrated hero.

Best to use two hero types to show conflict between two essentially good people with conflicting motivations to do good, that off-set each other.

2. **Crucible** = Nine people marooned in a small grocery store in a remote area by a raging blizzard. Things keep going wrong (electricity fails, no heat, people have accidents, etc)

Protagonist = local rancher who only wants to be a loner, reluctantly takes command because no one else will and he wants to survive.

Antagonist = man who has been paid to kill a woman who is hiding from her violently jealous ex-husband. But he only has her nickname, no picture, and he must discover if one of the women is his target.

3. Crucible = decrepit spaceship in deep space, surrounded by evil Company-owned planets and space stations, being chased by Company Liquidators:

Protagonist = Severn Baile, freelance thief whose unwarranted cocky confidence has put him on the Company hit list. Motivation = he wants to trick them into thinking they've killed him so he can decamp to the other side of the galaxy to hide and continue his carefree way of life.

Protagonist = Elya Paro, a runaway slave, the property of the Company, who has stowed away on Baile's ship. Motivation = to get home to her husband, the governor of Quantara and regain her safe, pampered life.

4. **Crucible** = an old three-story inn on an Atlantic barrier island in the middle of the largest hurricane to hit in recorded history.

Protagonist = A special agent of the US Marshal Office, sidelined by an injury, trying to run down a hired hit man. Motivation = if he doesn't kill the gunman, he will die, as will the woman he's fallen in love with.

Antagonist = the hired gun, a man who has never failed at a mission, who must find the mob's missing money or he won't get paid for this hit. Motivation = personal, way beyond his payment, because the agent and the woman have outwitted him thus far. He will not fail, ever. (This crucible became my suspense novel, *Sins of the Past*, available in print and as an ebook from Amazon.)

Lesson #5: The Horns of a Dilemma

Choice: #3, Spaceship Scene

Protagonist: Severn Baile: is basically a coward, wants everything his own way. Wants life to be an adventure so he doesn't have to deal with anything serious or adult.

Inner conflicts:

Inherent laziness vs his need to act and make decisions

Selfishness vs his growing love for Elya

Peter-pan syndrome vs emerging ability to think like an adult

His desire not to care vs caring so deeply it scares him

His deep belief he is not a good person vs his need to do good to redeem himself

His guilt over not being of use vs his need to hide until trouble goes away

His love of his robin hood lifestyle vs taking responsibility

Protagonist: Elya Paro: Once a sheltered, idealistic woman loved and pampered by her husband, kidnapped, tortured and enslaved by the Company as a "lesson" to her husband.

Inner conflicts:

Her desire for revenge vs her moral upbringing

Her yearning for her former life vs her knowledge she can never have it again

Her growing caring for Severn Baile vs her love for her husband

Her desire for revenge vs her need to do the right thing

Her hatred for the Company vs her moral roots

Her guilt over being the instrument of hurting her husband vs her shame over who she has become

Lesson #6: Character Development as Key to Conflict

Story: Destany's Daughter

Character: Meleia: a sheltered still-barely fifteen-year-old.

At the opening of the story, Meleia has been taught by her mother to be wary, but not the reasons for the need for caution. She knows she is different from other kids her age; for instance, her mother cannot leave the grounds surrounding their house. Meleia has become her mother's emissary with the outside world. She also knows her deceased father, who died before she was born, came from the dimension in which she lives, the 3rd, and that her mother came from the 4th dimension. But she doesn't understand the implications of that.

She knows that her mother is protecting her from danger and knows in what form the danger will arrive, but does not know the origins of the danger, nor the consequences of being caught in that danger. Her mother has promised to tell her everything in three years when she reaches eighteen. Meleia is sweet, basically trusting in the people she does know (classmates, trades people, teachers, etc) even with her mother's training. She understands what her mother says, but doesn't really believe it because she has never experienced betrayal at another's hands. She loves to read, lives in a fantasy world populated by characters from the stories in her books, dreams of being a heroine (like all teen girls her age), but runs from any true conflict.

From the time her mother dies at the very start of the story and Meleia's protection in gone, she is thrust into a world she neither wants nor understands. All that she believed in and depended on to make sense of her life has vanished, melted like ice in the desert. She is lied to at every turn, encounters situations that are beyond her ability to believe in much less understand, and she must learn somehow to find her inner core of strength if she is to survive.

I see her struggle starting in grief over her mother's death, and in fear, because of being taken away from her home and held captive by someone who claims he is her uncle. She wants to believe him despite the fact that he is the one who kidnapped her, but her mother's warnings keep ringing in her head. The more wary she is, the more angry and mean he becomes, further eroding her ability to trust him. When what she thinks of as magical things start happening, and she realizes she is no longer in her own dimension, she panics to the point of physically fighting against her uncle, who of course wins and buries her deeper in his aerie dungeon.

Meleia plots her escape the only way she can, by trusting the magical elements of this new world. Through this magic she is rescued by a young man, for whom she is a stand-in for a mother who was taken away by Meleia's uncle. He was too young to fight for her freedom, and uses freeing Meleia as a way to assuage his feelings of guilt. Once she is free, they argue and he abandons her to find her own way home, despite the fact that she has no idea where she is, or why her uncle is after her. This betrayal leads Meleia to conclude that people—at least in this dimension—are not reliable and she can count only on herself. She finds a trickle of inner strength that she hopes will carry her through until she reaches the portal that will take her through to her own dimension.

As she treks across this unknown, magic-ridden land, she encounters many people, some of whom help her, some of whom use her, and some who simply betray her for reward. And she hears rumors about herself, comes to eventually realize who she is and just why her uncle wants to control her. Each step along the way she learns more about who she is, who she wants to be, and what she will and will not tolerate. Through decisions that affect not only her life, but the lives (and deaths) of others, most of whom are innocents, she comes to terms with her own moral choices and bears the consequences of her actions with grace and stoicism. In other words, she grows up and becomes a very mature sixteen by the book's end.

Lesson #7: Opening Scene Tension

We had spent the afternoon in a cafe, a winter afternoon just like any other on Ladros. Soft flakes drifted down outside the window where we sat, masking the dirt and squalor of the city, muting the cacophony of life lived atop relentless machinery. The dome high above had vanished within the swirling snow. It gave me a sense of space, of freedom; we might have been back on Earth instead of on this sham of a rock.

Juddin Egralo now drank his coffee black, and my heart clenched each time he lifted the cup to his lips. Had we truly been apart so long that I was no longer privy to the changes in his life? I knew that time passed differently out here on the Perimeter, but it hurt to realize how much it had affected who we were.

I had loved him forever, Juddin Egralo, forever starting the day I'd met him in training. Since that was my second day of life, that's about as close to forever as I can get. I shudder to think how naive I was back then, how trusting, how excited I was to be part of the Unit. Reality lay before me, an obstacle course of disappointment and almost-mortal wounds that we all must overcome to survive. But Juddin saw something more in me, more than the Infiltrator I'd been designed to be. He'd taken my hand and led me to his room and showed me that life was more than a mission. When he'd finished destroying my ingrained insouciance, he'd kissed the top of my head and grinned.

"Not bad for a two-day-old," he'd said, his deep voice a velvet purr in the darkness. "I knew you were special. Meet me here tomorrow and we'll see how much you've learned overnight."

That was the beginning, and though for him it was merely a lark, teaching me how to live life and not just exist for the mission, for me it was food and drink for both body and soul. I'd have followed him anywhere—and pretty much did over the years. Each encounter added to the quiet joy that filled me just to look at him, at the broad shoulders and slim, tall frame, the arrowhead cheekbones and long red hair caressing his collarbones, the thin lips that vanished when he grew impatient or angry, the violet-blue eyes that saw things others missed. I existed for the missions and did my duty, but I lived for his touch. Then I lived just to see him after he threw me over for the next newborn.

And now we sat together after an absence of two Ladros years, long dry years without so much as a vid-call from him. I watched him drink his coffee black, watched the snow fall outside and listened to him craft the shape of my next mission. And I felt my heart shrivel in my breast as I gazed into Juddin's guileless blue eyes with Kannar's words echoing in my head: *Juddin Egralo is a double agent. Info confirmed. Your mission: Terminate him.*

Lesson #8: Handling Fear, Suspense and Terror

This is what I love, Cara thought as she let the steaming water stream over her head. *The entire hot water tank to myself*. It wasn't that she didn't love John and the boys, it was just that with a mechanic husband and three teenage boys in the house, hot water was always at a premium. And somehow she never had the coupon to redeem that premium.

Until tonight. John had taken their brood up to the mountains on an impromptu camping/fishing trip, leaving Cara to her own devices. She'd read the latest Ruth Rendell mystery, weeded the garden, had a shrimp salad for dinner—none of her men would touch the stuff so she rarely brought it into the house—and now she luxuriated beneath a glorious torrent of soothing warmth. *Life is good,* she thought.

She pulled her head back, wiped water from her face and picked up the bottle of expensive salon shampoo on which she'd splurged. A thud echoed through the closed door. Cara sighed.

"Elmer!" she yelled. "You dumb cat! If you knocked over my perfume bottle again I'm going to douse you in it!"

She listened and heard nothing, not even Elmer's usual answering yowl. Cara was sure that cat understood English—and thought she was speaking it back to her humans. He always mewed or yowled when spoken to. So why the silence now? What had he done that warrented silence?

"Elmer? Do I have to come out there?"

More silence. Then another thud, and a screech like rusty nails being torn from ancient wood. That was not Elmer. Cara froze, then parted the shower curtain just enough to peer at the bathroom door. Had she locked it? She couldn't remember turning the little knob, hadn't thought she needed to with the guys gone. She set the shampoo bottle down, then reached out and turned off the water.

She stood shivering in the cool air, listening with her whole body, but heard nothing more. She started to call out again, then stopped herself. If it wasn't Elmer, she didn't want to advertise her whereabouts. It was possible that the intruder hadn't heard the water running, depending on where he was in the house. If it was Elmer, she'd simply have to kill him once she gathered her wits together and warmed up enough to move.

A scrape echoed through the door. Cara jumped and almost slipped on the water-slick tub surface. It sounded like furniture being moved around, perhaps down the hall in the living room. Cara stepped from the tub and grabbed a towel, her mind sorting through her options. She'd been using the boys' bathroom because it was the biggest. That meant the nearest phone was either in the master bedroom or the living room. For the first time she found it quite unforunate that the master bedroom was off the living room, since that meant she'd have to go to the right, in the direction of the noises. Not smart.

What, then? She finished toweling herself off and slid on her robe. The boys' bedrooms lay to the left of the room she was in. If she headed there, she might be able to open a window and slink out without being caught. She'd be a sight running to the neighbors' house in her husband's plaid robe and her fuzzy kitty slippers, but she'd not let pride stand in the way of her safety.

She cracked the bathroom door and peered out into the hallway. Dark shadows hid any possible movement. Why hadn't she turned on some lights before stepping into the shower? She should have known better, especially after reading a Ruth Rendell tale. Another scrape and thud sounded from the living room, propelling her into the hall to the left. The closest of her boys' rooms it was.

She took no more than five steps before eerie movement near Jason's room froze her in place. A low grunt rolled toward her; glass shattered in the room behind the intruder. Cara caught a glimmer of light as the dark shadow stalked toward her. Her heart thudded. She could barely draw breath. She tried to speak, to plead for mercy, but the words strangled in her throat. She backed slowly down the hall toward the living room, pursued by the menacing phantom. Another appeared behind it, adding his deep growl to the threat.

Cara whimpered as she backed into the living room, certain she was about to be assaulted, perhaps killed. The noises behind her in the room grew louder: books sliding from the desk to the floor; a lamp crashing onto its side; furniture knocked askew on the hardwood floor. How many of them were there? What were they looking for? Where, damn it, was the phone?

Something—a chair arm, someone's hand?—snagged her robe and Cara screamed. All around her the dark shadows reared; the intruders screeched back at her. Cara hit at the nearest body, thrusting it aside. She raced through the gap toward the kitchen, barely aware of the cool breeze blowing in from sonewhere. She hit the light switch just inside the kitchen doorway and spun in a circle, seeking the phone. She snatched it up and dialled 9-1-1 as she ran toward the back sliding door.

It was open, only the screen stretched across the opening. A screen in which gaped a huge hole. Cara turned just as voice enquired about her emergency. She froze, blinked, then continued stepping slowly back toward the screen door and the deck outside.

"Yes, please, I need animal control. A pack of huge raccoons broke in through my back door and are running rampant in the house. Please, hurry!"

And just how was she going to explain to her four men that she'd left the deck door open while she took a shower in the dead of night?

Unit 10: Subplot

"Subplots should never lead the reader away from your theme and should, in fact, support your primary plot. A subplot happens because of (rather than instead of) the main story. Anything else is a distraction."

~Janalyn Voigt

WHY DO WE NEED subplots? First of all, most stories would feel thin and unrealistic without the addition of a subplot or two—or four or five. Subplots help round out the main story and make it feel complete. Subplots will, of course, add length (and pages) to your story, but they will also add the variety you need to keep readers interested. No writer wants readers who are disappointed that there wasn't more to the tale. Adding a subplot or two gives readers that sense of "more" without artificially loading the main plot with events that are boring or disconnected to the main action. Readers will then finish the book with a sense of fulfillment.

Subplots also help capture readers who might not be as interested in the main plot or the main characters—say, Jane and Dick Watson (yes, that happens!)—but who will read to the end to find out what happens to Aunt Sally and Cousin Marlon because they have bonded with those characters. A few good, intriguing subplots can help increase your audience.

Subplots can be found everywhere: in the movies and TV shows we watch and in the books we read. They can make stories even more exciting; we've experienced that excitement ourselves. Subplots add depth to characterizations and increase a reader's understanding of the story's main theme(s). But it isn't always easy when we sit down to write a story to even think up an appropriate subplot, much less seamlessly incorporate one, two or more into our narrative.

The purpose of a subplot is to **add to the main plot in a manner that is enlightening and meaningful** in some way. Subplots help draw readers into the story so deeply they have to continue turning pages. At least one subplot—and often more—is necessary to sustain depth and interest in a novel-length work. But even shorter pieces (other than flash fiction, which is too short to support anything other than a main plot) can benefit from a subplot that adds depth and realism, and helps sustain suspense and foreshadow the main events. Rule of thumb: short story (2,000 words and up) add only one subplot, if needed; long short story (over 10,000 words), two are okay; novellas and novels can carry two or three subplots; epics can hold 5 or more subplots in addition to the main plot. Flash fiction (under 2,000 words), no subplots, it's too short to support anything other than the main plot.

To be viable in your story, **subplots need to add to the main plot** in some way. A subplot **must** do **at least one** of the following:

1. **Add depth** to the main characters and help round out other characters in the story;

2. **Explore characters' desires**, goals, vulnerabilities, relationships, issues and/or growth as the story progresses;

3. **Affect or change the main plot**, and therefore the main characters, in a way that would not otherwise happen;

4. **Add variety** to help sustain interest in an ongoing main plot over the length of the novel or story;

5. **Reveal hidden or obscure meanings** and themes that add layers to the main story;

6. **Increase tension** by using cliffhanger points and a sense of mystery as the main plot and subplots continue to develop.

Subplots can be developed in parallel with the main plot, or be interwoven into it, structures we'll explore more fully. A subplot can also act as a mirror that reflects the main plot, it can drop clues that will affect the main plot at a later time, it can raise the stakes by adding complications, or it can provide comic relief. The following exercises will help you discover how to craft subplots that will ensure your story will not fall flat, or feel too one-note to readers.

By weaving a well-crafted subplot or two (or three!) into your story, you can add the kind of complexity and tension readers crave. And that will keep them coming back for more of your work.

Unit 10, Subplot: Contents

Lesson #1: From Situation to Subplot

SUBPLOTS THAT ARISE FROM the story itself are the easiest to weave successfully into the main plots of your stories. When the supporting plot arises organically from the main action in some way, it feels natural instead of intrusive to readers. And seamless integration is the goal for inserting a subplot or two into your narrative. Nothing can confuse or bore readers more than a subplot that has no connection to the main story line, no matter how well written it is.

A great place to find that necessary organic element is to study the story situation(s) in which your protagonist, supporting characters and antagonist find themselves. When you really look, you will be able to find many ways you can devise a subplot based on the main situation that can have an impact on the main plot in some unexpected way.

For example, take one of the subplots from my novel, *Tangled Webs*. It evolved because the main character's inherited car did not run. Because of this Lia is forced to stay in town, going to places she had hoped to avoid. She ends up at a new cafe and meets the owner, Andrea, and her husband and a friendship begins to grow. Andrea's trust and friendship bolsters Lia's courage, so that she is able to withstand the events that occur in the story's main plot. And their friendship helps show readers that the town's view of Lia is more than a little skewed.

The Andrea Subplot was not a conscious plan on my part when I first started writing the book. It grew out of the situation of the car not working. But when she met Andrea in the cafe, the subplot burst into life, deepening Lia's character and growth, her relationships, and reinforcing the main theme of the story.

One thing you want to be careful about when crafting your subplot(s) is to **not lose control** of them. That is, don't let a subplot become more important than, or overshadow, your main plot. Always remember that **the purpose of a subplot is to support the main plot**; if it doesn't, it has no place in your narrative. The bulk of the story, and the writing, must be around the main plot. A subplot must be interesting and intriguing, but it cannot take away from the main story line. It must, in some way, impact your protagonist—or antagonist.

The worst thing a writer can do is drop in a subplot that does not fit the story, that does not connect to the plot or main characters. The story of how Joe lost his uncle's cufflinks at his senior prom and spent the next decade trying to worm his way back into his uncle's good graces might be fun to write (though not necessarily to read!), but unless it somehow connects to Joe teaming with a detective to uncover the person who is embezzling funds at the bank Joe works at, it doesn't do anything to enhance the story. At best, these unconnected subplots are a distraction; at worst, they bore readers enough to put the story down unfinished. And no writer wants a dissatisfied reader.

Finding subplots that arise from the story's main situation will help ensure that they organically connect with the main plot line. And then they will do exactly what they are supposed to do: engage readers even more fully with your story and your characters.

Exercise #1: From Situation to Subplot*

(Purpose of Exercise: To find subplots in situations)

THIS EXERCISE HAS TWO parts and takes **forty-five minutes** to complete.

Write a scene between two or more people in which **something unexpected is revealed**. Now, consider what the main plot might be if you wrote the entire story, keeping in mind that the scene you just finished could be situated anywhere in the plotline. Write about 50 words synopsizing the plot. Give yourself **30 MINUTES** to do this part of the exercise, about 20 minutes for writing the scene and 10 for the plot outline.

After you finish the plot outline, go back and underline (or add) anything you think could be used as a possible subplot to the main story. Then answer these questions. How might these possible subplots evolve in the story? How would they interconnect with the main plot and/or characters? How would they reflect the theme of the main plot?

Take about **15 MINUTES** to finish this portion of the exercise.

Lesson #2: From the Past to Subplot

AS WE HAVE SEEN, the best subplots arise organically from the main story. Another place to look for this organic arising is within the characters themselves, the protagonist(s), supporting characters and antagonist(s).

Our characters do not come to life fully formed—though it may seem that way to us. But they have lives outside the confines of the story plot we devise for them. They are born into families of one kind or another, grow up, go to school, get jobs, fall in love, have wants and desires, likes and dislikes, just like we ourselves do. And somewhere within all that has happened to our characters, the things that make them who they are when the story starts, are the seeds of some amazing subplots that we might never think of on our own.

This is another strong reason to write a fully detailed biography of each of our main characters—protagonist(s), antagonist(s), sidekicks and other important characters who will populate the story. Take the Andrea Subplot from my novel *Tangled Webs*. Because I had written her biography, I knew that at one time Lia hoped to design quilted clothing. It was her outfit that first attracted Andrea to Lia. Had I not known Lia had once wanted to be a designer, I might have missed a wonderful subplot that helps readers understand and identify with her more fully. But because I had Lia dress in one of her own creations when she went to the cafe, Andrea was hooked and I discovered a subplot that helped deepen Lia's relationships and character.

Always remember, the things that happen to our characters in our main story plot **do not happen in a vacuum**. The characters have lives outside of the story events that intersect with and can impact positively or negatively what happens within the story line. And in those lives lie the seeds of what can be some very effective subplots.

Take, for example, a story outline I wrote in class: a sorcerer (Jarrod) and sorceress (Oraya) must fulfill a 1,000 year old prophecy by finding an object that will bring five warring planets into harmony. They are opposed by an evil coalition government headed by a man (Eslan) who is determined to retain power over the warring factions, which he will lose if peace is restored.

In the biography of my main protagonists, I discovered that the sorcerer Jarrod's powers arose when he lost his wife and three children in a highly technical bomb blast that destroyed his house. He worked with technology in his job at a forensic hospital, but has shunned it since the bombing. He was also once addicted to holo-horse racing. Oraya, a born sorceress, lives according to natural law but is willing to accept technological help when necessary. Her destiny goes far beyond simply locating that lost object, and beyond establishing peace for the planets. And when she was a child, she watched her brother drown.

Any of these things in my characters' backgrounds can serve as a subplot that will add conflict and complexity to the main story, the search for the mythical 5-sided Chalice of Unity. Jarrod's loss of his family and desire for vengeance can interfere with the quest he is on. His aversion to technology can cause tremendous difficulties for the pair as well as put them at odds with each other. His addictive personality can also add twists that take the pair into unknown situations. The same is true for Oraya's background. And also for that of the antagonist, Eslan, the titular head of the government.

This is an important point: **don't forget about your antagonist** when you search for subplots. Using pieces of your antagonist's background is one of the best ways to make that character more human to readers, and to throw obstacles in front of the character, as you weave a fascinating subplot around and through the main story. Remember, readers want their "villains" to be human, too, with the capacity to change and grow, even if they do not take advantage of the opportunity, or grow negatively instead of positively.

When you mine your characters' pasts for subplots, you draw readers more deeply into their stories because they will connect with the emotions and trials the characters have endured. Tapping into your characters' pasts for subplots makes them even more human to readers, because you will tap into emotions we all feel, and struggle with, at times. And when we connect with the characters' emotions, we bond with them.

Taking your subplots from the characters' lives will ensure that they will do their job by adding richness and complexity. The subplots will impact and affect those same characters, further enthralling readers. A win-win if ever there was one.

Exercise #2: From the Past to Subplot*

(Purpose of Exercise: To find subplots in the characters)

THIS EXERCISE HAS THREE parts and will take from about an hour to complete.

Part I: 20 Minutes

Write a scene between two people in an airport departure lounge. Concentrate on action and dialogue, and on creating lots of suspense and/ or tension. In other words, make this a compelling opening to a story. The time frame can be today, or in the past or future, as you choose.

Set your timer for **20 MINUTES** and start writing now.

Part II: 20 Minutes

Consider what the main plot might be if you finished the story. Write about 50 words synopsizing the plot. Then write about the main characters involved. Who are they? Give a short biography of them: age, marital status, kids, job, hobbies, character traits, etc.

Give yourself **20 MINUTES** to complete this portion of the exercise.

Part III: 15 Minutes

After you finish the bios, go back and underline anything you think could be used as a possible subplot to the main story. Then write the answers to these questions.

How might these possible subplots evolve in the story? How would they interconnect with the main plot and/or characters? How would they reflect the theme of the main plot? How could they help to sustain suspense or foreshadow the main events?

Set your timer for another **15 MINUTES** and begin this portion of the exercise now.

Lesson #3: From the Present to Subplot

SUBPLOTS CAN ALSO BE discovered in your characters' present lives, as well as in their pasts. The people who surround them, with whom they interact on a daily basis, and the choices they make because of these relationships, form perfect fodder for subplot devising.

People cultivate relationships in three main areas:

1. Private
2. Interpersonal
3. Professional

The **Private Relationship Area** is the place where we are true to who we really are. It's the 'me' we are when no one is looking, behind the closed doors of our house, the person only a very few trusted friends and/or family members ever see. In this area, we let our hair down, so to speak. We don't wear masks, don't try to be what we think we should be. We are totally exposed, warts and all. Only those who can be trusted with our deepest, darkest secrets ever get to see this 'rubber meets the road' person that we hide from the rest of the world.

The **Interpersonal Relationship Area** finds us wearing light masks in order to be 'presentable' to the rest of the world. This is where our more casual friends and acquaintances see the person we hope they will like. We adjust our reality to fit what we believe they want to see, and hide those things we are afraid will turn them away. We let them see only a portion of who we really are, the portion we hope they will like and accept. And often we will modify this portion of ourselves in order to be more like our friends and/or family, and thus be more accepted. When we do let out portions of our true persona, it is only those portions that have been carefully assessed for their compatibility factor.

In the **Professional Relationship Area** we wear heavy masks. This is who we are when we are at work, engaged in necessary daily activities, or working in a volunteer capacity—when we are interacting with the world at large. Sometimes the reality of who we are can be in direct opposition to the person we become in our Professional Relationship Area: the slob at home becomes an extremely organized bookkeeper or manager at work; the person who rarely reads because of his/her secret dyslexia becomes an avid advocate for literacy who teaches children the joy of reading in his/her volunteer position. The people around us are usually held at arm's length, often through fear that if anyone knew what or who we really were, they wouldn't like us. Or they would shun us. And so the reality of who we truly are is deeply hidden behind heavy masks that show the world only what we want it to see—most often it's what we think it wants to see.

Just from these descriptions of the three major life areas, it's easy to see how each can impact and complicate the others when they inadvertently intermingle. And complexity is what we are after with our subplots, because complexity makes things more difficult for our main characters, makes them strive even harder, and keeps readers turning pages. Complications keep our protagonists from reaching their story goal, which adds excitement and tension for readers. And that increases their interest and attention.

But remember that you can't just throw in any messy situation just because you found it in one of the three main relationship areas of your character's life. **All subplots**, even if they are about another character, **must impact your protagonist in some way**. They must enrich, deepen or advance the main plot, or reveal character motivation in a way that ultimately affects your main character(s).

And don't forget about your antagonist. That character, too, has a strong story goal—there wouldn't be anything for your protagonist to struggle against, and therefore no story at all, if the antagonist didn't have a strong story goal. Remember, this character's life doesn't exist in a vacuum any more than the protagonist's does. The antagonist's life also goes on while the story unfolds. It might be worth looking into your antagonists' Relationship Areas to see if there might be a subplot or two that will make their lives that much more difficult as they attempt to best your protagonists.

Mining the Private, Interpersonal and Professional Relationship areas of your main characters, both protagonists and antagonists, can provide a wealth of subplot material with which you can enrich and enhance your main plotlines. Use them with glee. After all, one good twist in a story deserves another, right?

Exercise #3: From the Present to Subplot*

(Purpose of Exercise: To discover subplots in life areas)

THIS THREE-PART EXERCISE SHOULD take less than an hour to complete.

Plotline: In a small town, a person starts a grass-roots movement to help save the endangered blue-spotted land turtle that is rapidly becoming extinct because of rampant expansion. This turtle's nesting ground is an exceptionally fertile and lovely 10-mile-wide plain that lies between the main employment district and most of the available housing in the area.

Step One: Write a short biography of three characters who might be involved in this story: who they are, their family, education, hobbies, etc. You can include the main character or not, as you choose. **Important:** For all three characters, **include details about their private, interpersonal and professional lives.** Give yourself **20 minutes** for this step.

Step Two: Now, **for each character**, write out a short description of a possible subplot that is formed from one of these three relationship areas: his or her private, interpersonal or professional life. You should end up with one subplot for each character, with each subplot based on one of the main relationship subplot areas: **private, interpersonal, professional**. Consider carefully for each character which of the three areas is best suited for the subplot involving that character, for not all areas of relationship for each character will yield a great subplot for the mail story line. Give yourself about **20 minutes** for this step.

Step Three: When you finish, pick your favorite subplot. Now, consider that the new **main plot** of the story (it may end up having nothing to do with the original given plotline). For **15 minutes**, brainstorm other subplots that could be used in conjunction with this new main story line.

Lesson #4: From the Future to Subplot

ANOTHER GREAT PLACE TO uncover subplots is in the future of your characters. By the future I mean the goals your characters set for themselves in life, things they want or need to accomplish at some point in the future—a day, a month, a year, a decade, etc. A direct benefit of mining your character's life goals to uncover subplots is that they will arise organically from who your character is, rather than feel contrived or stuck in the narrative simply to fill up space or add length.

There are three areas where people have goals for their lives and, of course, our characters will also have those same three areas in their lives. These "ordinary" goals will naturally be outside the scope of the main plot, so you will have to make sure they connect to the main plot in some way. This should not be very difficult to do because these goals are intrinsic to the character's life.

When you map out these life goals for your character, be sure to look for **those that will most complicate the main plotline**; that is, those that will enrich, deepen and help advance the main plot and/or will reveal the character's motivation. Eliminate all those that are merely messy situations or that don't impact the main plot.

There are three kinds of life goals:

1. Daily goals
2. Short-term Goals
3. Long-term Goals

Daily Goals are the small tasks that need to be accomplished as part of daily life: grocery shopping, finding a mechanic to do an oil change on the car, taking the cat to the vet, picking up the kids from school. This is probably the least promising area for subplot material, though with the right story, a daily task can complicate the main plot. For example, you might have a story about a cop who is busy investigating a high-profile murder. But since his wife is away for six months in the military, he has to be available every day at 3:15 pm to pick up his kids from school. Such a subplot could complicate the main plot by interfering with witness and suspect interviews and following up on clues, and it could show both the character's devotion to family and his ability—or inability—to juggle two difficult tasks.

Short-term Goals are things that one hopes to accomplish within a short time-frame—a few days or weeks, or even a few months. The character may have a presentation due at work, one that will ensure he does not lose his job, or the goal of remaining sober for the next six months to prove to his estranged wife that he is determined to win her back. Short-term goals offer more room for subplots, as they have a longer "shelf life," as it were. They last for a more extended period of time, and are usually of more import for the character than daily goals. For example, that same cop who is immersed in the high-profile case might have to take a second job in order to pay for this daughter's college tuition, which puts his marriage in jeopardy. This kind of distraction would definitely impact his ability to concentrate on the case, and how he handles the stress would tell readers a lot about his character.

Lastly we have **Long-term Goals**, those far-reaching plans that must be worked toward but often will not come to fruition for many years. These present a smorgasbord of choices for subplots because the stakes are a lot higher for the characters if they do not achieve these goals. They stand to lose much more, and may therefore be willing to do a lot more—or give up a lot more—to find success. Learning to walk again after a serious accident, saving enough money to purchase a home, raising healthy, well-adjusted children, earning a Ph.D. degree after one's children have left the nest are all examples of long-term goals. They take more care, more planning and loom larger in our lives than our daily or short-term goals, even though they seem to be on the "back burner" compared to our daily activities. A long-term goal becomes the lodestone toward which we turn constant, if often subconscious, attention, and around which we fashion our lives until it is reached.

Think about our busy homicide detective, immersed in that high-profile murder that must be solved quickly. Now give him a long-term goal , a burning desire to someday retire to a life of leisure in the South Seas even though he's not able to put aside much money. Such a long-term goal could complicate the main plot by perhaps having a character offer him a sizable bribe. The detective will have to choose between his goal of affording his dream and staying true to the laws he swore to uphold. This could impact the main plot in any number of ways depending on who is offering the bribe, and what the cop is being asked to overlook.

The important thing to remember when it comes to subplots based on a character's goals, whether daily, short-term or long-term ones, is that **the subplot must connect to the main plot in some way**. It doesn't have to have a huge impact, but it must connect somehow, or at worst all you have is a boring tangent to the main story that makes readers put the book down, and at best, a well-written excursion that merely confuses readers as to why it's there. It might be fun to write about the detective smashing up his father's Dodge DeSoto after the junior prom, but unless that event has a bearing in some way on the case he is investigating, it has no place in the story.

This means that even if the subplot revolves around a secondary character—which also adds depth and richness to the story—it still must complicate the main plot, must affect your protagonist in a way that makes it harder for him or her to reach the story goal. It doesn't matter that your protagonist's best friend stole a bike in seventh grade and your protagonist didn't turn him in, unless that event somehow triggers or complicates some aspect of the main plot.

Look at the life goals of all your characters—your protagonist, your secondary characters, and your antagonist—and then brainstorm subplot ideas based on who they are and what they want out of life, what their future goals are. Then analyze those ideas to see **which complicates your hero's life the most**. The idea here is to make it as hard as possible for your protagonist to reach that story goal. Keep in mind that great subplots that are carefully crafted from your characters' lives can turn a good novel into a great one.

Make your subplots exciting and interesting. Make them deep and introspective. Sprinkle clues to the main plot into them, or let them stand as comic relief. But most of all, if nothing else, make sure they connect to the main plot, that they complicate the protagonist's life in some way and deepen motivations. Then you'll have a rich, exciting story that can't be put down.

Exercise #4: From the Future to Subplot*

(Purpose of Exercise: To discover subplots in characters' life goals)

THIS THREE-PART EXERCISE SHOULD take about an hour to complete.

Step One: Take the main character from a story you are working on, or choose one of the characters you created for the previous exercise. Write out the story goal for that character at the top of your page. Then brainstorm at least three possible life goals for **each** of the three main areas for this character: Daily, Short-term, Long-term. (You should have 3 or more daily goals, 3 or more short-term goals and 3 or more long-term goals). Then choose **one from each area** and craft the outline of a possible subplot that will complicate the story goal of this character. This is not a scene, just an outline of the subplot. Remember that each subplot must connect to the main plot in some way. Give yourself **20 minutes** for this step.

Step Two: Now, choose another character from the same story—the antagonist or a secondary character—or choose another character from the previous exercise, and brainstorm at least 3 life goals for that character in each of the three areas. When you finish, choose the best from **each** area and craft possible subplots that will complicate the story goal of the **main character** even though this subplot revolves around the antagonist or a secondary character. (Remember, all subplots need to complicate the protagonist's life in some way.) Set your timer for **20 minutes** for this step.

Step Three: Now consider the main plot of the story and the goal of the main character. Look over the three subplots from each of the characters in Step One and Step Two, then choose **one subplot from each** that you feel will most complicate your main character's life, the ones that will best interfere with the achievement of the story goal. Write out how these two subplots will impact the main plot. Give yourself **20 minutes** for this step.

Lesson #5: Other Subplot Sparkers

THERE ARE OTHER WAYS to devise subplots for your stories, ways not necessarily connected to the past, present or future of your main character. While of necessity all the subplots must connect to the main plot, other areas of the story can also be fertile ground for subplot ideas. I call them Subplot Sparkers.

Sparkers come from the fringes of life, from characters' motivations, from connections between people, and other areas. Being aware of these other places where subplots can lurk will help you discover some really fun or thoughtful subplots that you might not otherwise consider.

There are seven areas you can mine for extra subplots:

1. Who Else Has an Agenda? Consider all the characters in your story and see if any have a hidden agenda that might impact the direction of the main plot. Remember that **not all your characters will have the same goal as your protagonist**. Or your antagonist. The protagonist's best friend could be against what he/she wants or needs to do. There could be rivals waiting to throw a monkey wrench into well-laid plans. There might even be a traitor or two among the supporting cast of characters. Give them all a good long look to see who else—

besides the antagonist—has an agenda that conflicts with the main character's actions.

2. Main Plot Ripples. Every decision the main character makes will have repercussions among his family, friends, acquaintances and even strangers. People will have opinions, will want to insert their "two cents," or will be affected either positively or negatively by what your character thinks, says, decides and does. Consider who else in the story will be impacted by your protagonist's choices, and how that impact could affect the main plot.

3. The Hero's Vulnerabilities or Foibles. Readers expect characters who are strong and capable, but who are also human. The best way to make your character human is to give that character a vulnerability or flaw. And to get the most out of the vulnerability or flaw, design it so it interferes with and complicates the main plot. If your story is about a young girl striving to become a singing star, give her severe stage fright or make her tone deaf. If your story is about a firefighter in New York City's highrises, make him terrified of heights. (Don't forget your antagonist. A character flaw will help make that character human, also.)

4. Add Romance. If you create a subplot of romantic interest for a non-romantic story, you add a further dimension to the story. Look for attractions among your characters, especially among those who should not become involved, and you'll instantly add sizzle and tension. For example, the detective investigating a bank robbery could be drawn to a teller who is married to one of the robbers. Or he might be attracted to his partner's wife. A love triangle that simmers in the background of the main plot will immediately raise the stakes for at least three characters. Be sure to keep a tight rein on this kind of complication, though, or you'll stray into the romance genre. In this case, less is definitely more.

5. Lighten Up. Check your characters and situations for the lighter, humorous side of life, which can make for some great subplots. Adding humor is a great way to offset the tension of a heavily dramatic story and give readers a chance to breathe before they plunge back into the nail-biting excitement. The caveat here is to make sure the humor blends with the story line and isn't just thrown in there for effect, or you'll have scenes that stop readers cold. For example, you could have the protagonist's best friend be someone who continually spouts malapropisms (for example, instead of saying, "That's where the rubber meets the road," he or she might state, "That's where the rubber ball bounces on the road."), thereby adding humor and breaking tension.

6. Supporting Characters. These are the characters who are just under the secondary characters in importance to the story. They are more than walk-on characters, but don't take on the full burden that best-friend or sidekick-type characters do. Sometimes the perfect subplot is waiting in these characters' lives as you explore their storyline. Just be very careful not to let these subplots overshadow the main plot or the protagonist. Prudent connecting to the main plot is the secret when blending in a supporting character's subplot.

7. Theme/Message. You can use a subplot to blend a message or theme into the storyline. It won't work for every genre, but many will lend itself to incorporating views on environmentalism, politics, morality or philosophy into the plot. But **be very careful not to allow the message to override the main plot**. The story is the point of the book; if there is no main plot—or a too-buried main plot—there is no story. Never forget you are writing fiction. **The point is to entertain** readers; they can turn to nonfiction if they want facts and data. Keep the message subtle and connected to the main plot and readers will enjoy it as part of the story.

Finding subplots in your stories can be a lot of fun. And they will add interest and fun for readers, too. Finding subplots in the elements of the story makes them that much more integrated and believable. And that's a win-win all around.

Exercise #5: Other Subplot Sparkers*

(Purpose of Exercise: To Explore Other Ways to Find Subplots)

THINK OF A STORY you are writing, or use a story idea from previous exercises. Write out a short description of the main plot. List the protagonist and antagonist, the other main characters and the supporting characters.

Now consider these characters and the situations in the story and search out ideas for subplots using the Subplot Sparkers:

1. Who Else Has an Agenda?
2. Main Plot Ripples
3. Hero's Vulnerabilities/Foibles
4. Add Romance
5. Lighten Up
6. Supporting Characters
7. Message/Theme

Try to find **at least one** subplot in **each** of the 7 Subplot Sparkers areas in your story. (This may not be possible with a couple of them depending on the genre of your story.) How might each subplot add to or complicate the main plot of the story?

Give yourself **45 minutes** to finish this exercise.

Lesson #6: The Linear Subplot

THERE ARE TWO MAIN types of subplot structures: **Linear and Interwoven**. Consider all of them for your stories. You don't want all your subplots to be the same. You need variety in the structure of your subplots just as you need in your scenes and your sentences. Variety adds a sense of tension, which increases excitement, eliminates boredom and keeps readers turning pages.

The **first type of Linear plot is the Parallel Plot**. It runs alongside the main plot. It can remain separate all the way through, never touching the main plot, or the two plots can converge toward the end of the story. But, even though the two plots don't touch for most or all of the story, that doesn't mean the subplot does not have an impact on the main plot in some way.

Parallel plots are especially useful for thrillers, mysteries, suspense and young adult (YA) tales. The amount of "real estate," or exposure, the subplot has depends on how minor or major it is relevant to your main plot.

Here's an example: in my suspense novel, *Piece By Piece*, we have the main story of Julie in Buffalo, New York, and her life after she meets Ken. But the story shifts every few chapters to the subplot of Ogden

Wilkes in Harrisburg, Pennsylvania, and his relationship with two other men (subplot #1) and to the story of the Cortaid family (subplot #2). Not until the last few chapters of the story do these two subplots merge with the main plot and the connection between them comes clear.

Using this type of subplot, you can switch from protagonist to antagonist and allow readers to spend an extended period of time with each, a chapter or more. Parallel subplots let you develop motivations, reveal character and detail necessary backstory that might otherwise need to be left out, or spread out in such small pieces it would be hard for readers to follow. Parallel subplots are also a great way to keep readers guessing: what does Amy's attraction to her boss at her new job have to do with Nicole winning the beauty pageant? Readers will keep turning pages to discover the answer.

The key, of course, is to **drop subtle clues** throughout both plots so when the connection is finally revealed, readers say, "Oh, yes, that's why she did this, and he said that. I should have guessed." You can't just hook two interesting stories together by forcing a connection that isn't intrinsic to the story and characters. **The connection must be real and must make sense**, or you'll lose your audience. And no writer wants that to happen.

The **second type of Linear plot is the Bookend Subplot**. To use this technique, you introduce a subplot early on, then more or less leave it alone until the end, where it is resolved and connected to the main plot. This can be done before or after the main plot is resolved. Saving a subplot to wrap up after the main plot is done gives readers some breathing space after the emotion of the climax, a place where they can quietly enjoy that order has been restored, justice has been served, Kate and Jim are headed for happily ever after, or whatever.

A Bookend Subplot works like this: You have a story about a wealthy, powerful man who drinks too much and makes life hell for his family. But he gets away with it because he is rich and has connections. Near the beginning of the story, insert a scene where this man, drunk at 2:00 in the afternoon, takes a rake and beats at the young man who works for the lawn service because he is not mowing the lawn in straight enough lines. By the end of the book, readers will have pretty much forgotten about that young man, then up he pops again, now graduated from law school and sitting as a judge in the court before which the drunk is hauled for yet another DUI. The man's fate is now up to this kid. Payback... and isn't it sweet?

For best results, try to insert a little foreshadowing somewhere in the middle of the story. For the above example, you might craft a scene where the wife calls and asks the lawn service what happened to that nice young man who did such a good job on the mowing and trimming, only to be told he quit—to go to law school.

Linear Subplots work really well with first-person-narrated main plots. They allow you to narrate events that the first person narrator couldn't know by making those events part of the subplot and telling the Linear Subplot through another character's POV. (Narrate the subplot in third person, not first; two first person narrators are confusing. See *Volume 2, POV* for a full explanation.) This does not confuse readers, because the plots do not intermingle. The parallel nature of the plots keeps the two plot arcs well separated and easily understandable.

With the right story, a Parallel or Bookend type subplot might be just what you need to add the interest, intrigue and compelling elements necessary to sustain reader interest.

Exercise #6: The Linear Subplot

(Purpose of Exercise: To explore crafting Linear Subplots)

THIS EXERCISE HAS THREE parts. It should take about an hour to finish.

PART ONE: Choose a story you are working on, create a new one, or use one of the story ideas from a previous exercise. Or use the main plot idea below.

Write out the **main plot** of your story or use this one: While trapped on a vacation island by a hurricane, a curmudgeonly artist is found murdered. When Jane discovers he is her mother's former lover who recently reappeared in her life, and her father is accused of murdering the man, Jane decides she has to find the real murderer and free her father of suspicion. Now ask yourself: What other characters populate this story, and what is the role of each in the story (ex: antagonist, best friend, lover, etc.)?

Give yourself **15 minutes** for this part.

PART TWO: When you finish Part One, think up a subplot that could run in **parallel** with the main plot. What is that Parallel Subplot, and how will it impact the main plot? At what point will it merge with the main plot, or if it doesn't, why not? What affect will this Parallel Subplot have on the protagonist, and what will change for the protagonist because of this subplot?

Set your timer for **20 minutes** for this part of the exercise.

PART THREE: Now think of a possible Bookend Subplot you could have in this story. How will the subplot begin, how will it end, and what clue or clues will you insert in the middle to help strangthen the connection between the beginning and the ending? What effect will this Bookend Subplot have on the main plot and the protagonist?

Take **20 minutes** to finish this part of the exercise.

Lesson #7: The Interwoven Subplot

A STORY SHOULD BE like a slice of real life, but without all the boring and non-sequential parts that consume so much of our days. It should feel like real life to readers, but can't actually be a faithful depiction of real life or we'd bore our audience right to sleep.

When we interweave subplots around and through the main plot of our story, we in effect create that "slice of life" feel while keeping things interesting and exciting for readers. That is because the subplots, while adding depth and richness, also connect to and illuminate the main plot. When we multi-layer our stories, we add the verisimilitude that readers crave.

There are **two types of Interwoven subplots,** the **Tapestry Subplot** and what I call the **Hopscotch Subplot**.

Tapestry Subplots weave together like the threads of a tapestry to form a complete picture. Tapestry Subplots are interwoven into the story almost from the very beginning. Once the main plot and the subplot connect, they interact with each other for the entire length of the story, each affecting and impacting each other. If you have only a main plot and one subplot, think of it like a twisted rope. If you have a main plot and two or more subplots, you can liken it to a braid.

Here's how a **Tapestry Subplot** works.

Main plot: (Jane's POV) Jane's father is accused of killing her mother's former lover, the man she once had a torrid affair with earlier in her marriage. The ex-lover has recently reappeared in their lives. But Jane is convinced her father would never kill anyone, not even the man who was his rival for his wife's affections, so, with her best friend, she sets out to prove her father innocent by finding the real killer.

Subplot #1: (William's POV) Jane's boyfriend, William, who Jane is thinking of marrying, is disenchanted with her family. When he learns of Jane's quest, he becomes afraid for Jane's safety and flies into town. He sets out take control of Jane and to stop her sleuthing. He distracts her with romance, argues logic to change her mind, picks fights with her, and eventually challenges her to choose between him and crime solving.

Subplot #2: (Detective's POV) The detective, who is convinced that Jane's father is guilty, has problems of his own. His sixteen-year-old daughter has been refusing to do homework, skipping school and sneaking out of the house at night when her parents are asleep. Nothing the detective does has any effect other than to make matters worse. The detective's feelings of being a failure as a parent serve to make him more inflexible on the job because he's determined to be the best damned detective in the world since it's obvious to him that's all he's good at.

The three plots start out separately—chapter one could be Jane arguing with the cops and the prosecutor about her father's innocence, then detrmining to find the real killer herself (main plot); chapter two could be her phone conversation with William and his flight into town where he hopes to convince Jane to abandon her father and leave town with him (subplot #1); chapter three might be about the detective confronting his daughter as she tries to sneak back into the house at 6:00 a.m. and ending up feeling like a failure who has only one sure thing in life, his ability to capture the bad guys (subplot #2). But then the plots begin to merge. William reaches town and begins to undermine Jane, who is trying to figure out how to prove her father's innocence. The detective goes from being called on the carpet for inattention to his job because of his daughter, to an interview with Jane who he thinks wants to meddle in his case and prove him inept in his job. And the story goes on from there, with the plots intermingling, sometimes in the same chapter with line breaks to denote the change, and sometimes as full chapters of their own.

Tapestry Subplots merge into the main plot near the beginning of the story, and weave through the entire story until the end. **Hopscotch Subplots**, however, are similar to the game of hopscotch; they **hop in and out of the main plot**, first lying alongside it like a parallel subplot for a few chapters, then merginging with the main plot for a chapter or two, only to hop away again and maintain a parallel position before hopping back to touch the main plot. In a Hopscotch Subplot, the parallel parts can narrated or not, as needed. Sometimes all readers see are the places where the plots actually touch.

A good example of a Hopscotch Subplot is the hired killer subplot in my suspense novel, *Piece By Piece* (spoiler alert here for those who haven't read it yet). We first see Bernard Maximilian Keel when he is on the phone with the person who hired him (who is not revealed until near the end). He has no face-to-face contact with his target other than his visual from the phone booth as she walks past him down the street. A few chapters later, we are again with Keel, who secrets himself in a deserted building, puts together a rifle, then sights in on his target and shoots (and misses). Again, no face-to-face, overt contact with the target. The next time we see Keel, a few chapters later, is when he physically attacks his target who fights back and bests him. A few chapters later we find Keel in a hospital where he dies, thus ending the subplot—except for the brief mention near the end about who had hired him in the first place. Though its strand interweaves through the story, all we see of this Hopscotch Subplot is the places where it touches and affects the main plot, the places where the strand comes to the front of the tapestry and is visible to the eye.

Whether you braid all your subplots into the main plot for the length of the novel, creating a tapestry, or braid most and let one Hopscotch through the pages, interwoven subplots will give readers a sense of complete immersion in the lives of the characters who people the story. And when readers are immersed, they can't put the book down. Plus, they will want more when they do finish the story and go on to your next book. And your next. What writer could want more that that?

Exercise #7: The Interwoven Subplot

(Purpose of Exercise: To explore crafting interwoven Subplots)

THIS EXERCISE HAS THREE parts. It should take about an hour to finish.

PART ONE: Choose a story you are working on, create a new one, or use one of the story ideas from a previous exercise. Or use the main plot below.

Write out the main plot of the story (or use this one: Ben and Christa have been married for eleven years, and things seem to be cooling off between them. Then Ben comes home from work and says he has accepted a promotion which requires them to move across the country, away from friends and the family Christa depends upon.) What other characters populate this story, and what is the role of each in the story (ex: antagonist, best friend, lover, etc.)?

Give yourself **15 minutes** for this part.

PART TWO: When you finish Part One, think up a subplot that would interweave like a tapestry with the main plot. What is that Tapestry Subplot, and how will it impact the main plot? How does the way it interweaves impact the plot and characters? What effect will this Tapestry Subplot have on the protagonist, and what will change for the protagonist because of this subplot?

Set your timer for **20 minutes** for this part of the exercise.

PART THREE: Now think of a possible Hopscotch Subplot you could have in this story. How will the subplot begin, where and how many times will it "hop" in to touch the main plot? Will the parallel parts be narrated or invisible? What effect will this Hopscotch Subplot have on the main plot and the protagonist?

Take **20 minutes** to finish this part of the exercise.

Lesson #8: Ongoing Subplots

IF YOU ARE CONSIDERING writing a sequel or series, or merely want to leave the door open to the possibility, you need to leave something open, or unresolved, at the end of the story that will lure readers on. Subplots are perfect for leading readers into the next installment of the story. It's a lot like the way shows on TV are "spun off" the original show.

We're all familiar with the "spin off" phenomenon from television and even movies. If you remember the old TV series, *The Mary Tyler Moore Show*, in 1974 a subplot story was spun off as *Rhoda* so Mary Richards' best friend, Rhoda, could continue her story on her own. In the sci-fi realm, *Angel* spun off from *Buffy the Vampire Slayer* in 1999 to satisfy those who wanted to know what happened to him after the vampire with a soul left Sunnydale. From the original *Star Trek* has come a variety of shows: *TNG*, *Deep Space 9*, and the prequel *Enterprise*. The *Law and Order* mega-series began with the original show and grew to include *Special Victims Unit* (debuted in 1999 and still going strong), *Criminal Intent, Trial By Jury* and *LA* (as well as sister shows in the UK, France and Russia) and the *NCIS* group has multiplied to include venues in Washington, Los Angeles and now New Orleans.

Subplots can work the same way for writers, as spinoffs. Devise an interesting subplot for a story titled, say, *New Orleans Gumbo* about Belle's adventures in the French Quarter when she visits her Uncle Joe, and readers may clamor for more about Uncle Joe, prompting you to begin a series about his individual story after Belle goes home. Or maybe it's just your creative mind that starts pushing with more ideas for Uncle Joe and his life, apart from what had happened with his niece Belle. Now you have a whole other book (or even a new series) you might never have thought of without the impetus of that little subplot.

It's subplots that fill the bill when you are looking for a way to move into a series (or if you simply want to keep the door "ajar" in case you decide to someday head in that direction). **Never make the mistake of leaving the main plot unresolved**. It might seem like a great way to entice readers to purchase and read the next book in the series, but nothing annoys readers more than getting to the end of a book and discovering that they're being manipulated into having to get the next volume in order to find out what happens in the main plot. It's probably happened to you; I know it's happened to me more than once. And trust me, I was not a happy camper. (Nor did I get that next book!)

Readers don't want to be **forced** into purchasing or reading another book to find out what happens in the main story line. They want to be intrigued enough to **choose for themselves** whether or not to purchase and read the next volume in the series. Only by tying up the main plot but **leaving one of the subplots open** can you create the combination of satisfaction and intrigue that will prompt readers to pick up that next volume.

Take the example of the homicide detective investigating that high-profile murder case (main plot), with the daughter in college and his marriage in trouble (sub plots). You chose the book because the main plot intrigued you; you want to know about the murder: how it happened, who did it, and if and how they're caught. Imagine how angry you'd be if, after 200-some pages, the book ends before the mystery is solved. All that time you spent reading and you still don't know what happened. Or who did it. And now you have to buy another book, with no guarantee that one will wrap up the main plot, either. Maybe you'll have to buy a third book before you find out. Or a fourth. Will you bother? Probably—like me—you'll stop with volume #1 and vow never to read that author again.

If it's happened to you, you know how disappointed and even angry you felt. Your readers will be equally angry if you do that to them, because they'll feel cheated. And manipulated. No one likes feeling manipulated; it leads to resentment. What will happen instead of readers getting the next book in the series is that they won't purchase any more of your books at all.

But if the mystery—or the main plot—that first intrigued them is solved or wrapped up by the end of the first book, readers will be happy. They'll feel satisfied and glad they read the book. Then, if the detective's marriage is still in trouble or there's an ongoing problem with the daughter in college (or whatever subplot is left hanging), and readers have come to care about these characters (as you hope they will), they will want to go on to the next book, where another fun mystery (or main plot) is waiting along with more in the ongoing saga of the detective's personal life.

Another example is my in-progress paranormal Skylark Detective series. Each short story, novella or novel revolves around a murder my detective, Skylark, must solve. And each story wraps up with the mystery solved. But Skylark's personal story continues through each of the pieces. She was abandoned at birth accompanied by a cryptic note and a skylark pendant on a chain. That's all she knows. Who Skylark is—the story of her past, her oftentimes reluctant search for her roots and her need to know where her paranormal abilities come from—forms the base of the ongoing subplot I hope will intrigue readers enough to continue reading through the series as they enjoy each of the major plot mysteries.

Most often it's a personal life subplot that will intrigue and draw readers on to the second book, the third, and so on (along, of course, with your excellent writing and story telling skills), though it doesn't have to be, depending on the story. One caveat here: If you're not sure you want to do a series but want to simply leave the door open to the possibility, leave one of the **minor** subplots unresolved, not one of the larger, more important ones. Or simply drop **a one or two sentence teaser** at the end, the way I did with Proof of Identity: *Surely whatever was in there could never get out. Could it?* Then, if you never do write the sequel or series, readers won't be too disappointed at what was left hanging.

Analyze your subplots carefully to find just the right one to carry readers into the next volume. Readers will make the choice to continue with your ongoing saga because they care about the characters and want to know more about the ongoing subplot. They won't feel cheated or that they "have to" continue just to find out how the main plot ends in each volume, because every main plot is nicely wrapped up for them, bow and all. And that gives them a feeling of satisfaction even as the ongoing subplot lures them on.

When that happens, you've gained a reader for life, rather than turned readers off.

Exercise #8: Ongoing Subplots

(Purpose of Exercise: To identify subplots that can form
the base of an ongoing series)

THIS EXERCISE IS IN two parts. It should take about **45 minutes** to complete.

Part One: Choose a story you're working on, or use one of the ones you devised for a previous exercise. Wrte out a description of the main plot and how it is wrapped up at the end.

When you finish that, list all the subplots that are used, or brainstorm ones that could be used, in the story. Note how those subplots impact and affect the main character.

Take **20 minutes** to complete this part of the exercise.

Part Two: Analyze each subplot for its level of importance in the story and rank them as the most important being #1, on down to the least important. Beside each, note down the possible result of leaving each subplot unresolved. Try to become the "reader" and gauge your reaction to not knowing how the subplot wraps up.

Once you have done that, choose which subplot you feel would best lure readers on to the next volume. Do you anticipate a sequel, a trilogy or a full series? Will the subplot chosen support a sequel or trilogy? Is the subplot chosen strong enough to sustain interest past a sequel/trilogy, into a series? If not, which other subplot might be better for an ongoing series?

Set your timer for **20 minutes** and start now.

Lesson #9: Subplot or Main Plot?

WHEN WE'RE IN THE throes of creating a story, sometimes it's hard to tell when something is a complete subplot of its own, or if it's simply part of the main plot. The rule of thumb is if it stars the main character, it's probably an aspect of the main plot. If it centers around a secondary character whose actions impact the main character in some way, changing or pushing the main plot, it's probably a subplot.

But some subplots are subtle enough to make them hard to recognize as subplots, and some aspects of the main plot can sometimes feel more like subplots. That's why it's important to know the **story arc** of your main plot and each of your subplots. Take the time to write out the story arc for each of your plots, main and sub-. Then analyze those arcs. Those pieces that have the same story arc belong together as one plotline. Those that have unique arcs can stand alone. Once you have identified the elements of the main plot and the subplots, you can then decide which subplot structure for each subplot will best serve the story you need to tell.

This is an important step to take in the planning of your story. It helps you organize your thoughts, plan your timeline of events, determine the best ways to integrate your subplots, and discover any holes or problems that may need another subplot, or an alteration of an existing one, to plug or solve. By seeing how the main plot and subplots interact before you begin the actual writing, you can make sure that the tension rises dramatically throughout the story and transformative forces spur growth, gain, corruption or loss; the action pivots with unexpected twists that make it harder for the main character to attain his/her story goal; speed up or slow down the pacing as needed, and more.

When crafting the story arc for your subplots, ask what you want to accomplish with that particular subplot. What does the story need from it? How will it impact the main plot and change things for the protagonist? And don't forget to consider what you want in the story, what would be fun for you to explore and work with. After all, you have to spend a lot of time in this world and with these characters. Make sure you design it so you'll want to be in their company for an extended period of time. Readers may spend anywhere from a day to a week in your story world, communing with your characters, depending on how fast they read. But you might be caught in there with them for a year, or two or three. So make it a place you really want to be.

Remember, too, when crafting your subplots, that their main purpose is to make things difficult for your main character. If your main plot feels flat or stalled, or if you get a one-note vibe from it, don't despair. Simply sit down with the main plot's story arc and brainstorm what other people could populate that world, and how they might cause problems for your hero. Then pick the best of them and craft and weave in those subplots to advance the story in satisfying increments.

Exercise #9: Subplot or Main Plot?

(Purpose of Exercise: to learn to recognize which elements belong to the main plot or subplots)

THE PLOTLINES LISTED BELOW are from my in-progress fantasy novel titled *Stealing Shyon*. Read each one and decide which one or ones form the main plot of the story. Who is the protagonist? Who is the antagonist? Write out the story arc for the main plot, the protagonist's story goal, and mark which plotlines belong to the main story.

Now look at the remaining plotlines and determine the story arcs for each. Are any the same or nearly the same? Can any be combined together as one subplot? Which stand on their own? Group those that you feel belong together, then write a story arc/goal for each identified subplot.

Plotline #1: Queen Amalia of Shyon, barely out of her teens, works to be a benevolent queen

Plotline #2: Queen Amalia is kidnapped and held in isolation until she gives up Shyon

Plotline #3: Karina, Amalia's sister, falls in love with Prince Mendrick of Bair

Plotline #4: Prince Mendrick of Bair plots to steal Shyon for himself

Plotline #5: Prince Terren of Kladdis has no intention of marrying, although by law he must once he is crowned King of Kladdis in a few months

Plotline #6: Little Lord Keldin learns the secrets of the Shyon court and has to figure out what to do with them to help the missing Queen

Plotline #7: Daigard, a Kladdan outlaw, decides to climb Fire Mountain and retrieve the Orb of Destiny so he will gain power and prestige

Plotline #8: Princess Karina's unmarried handmaid, Rella, discovers she is pregnant and must deal with the disgrace

Plotline #9: The Sorceress Testra falls in love with Daigard and wants him for her own

Plotline #10: The Wizard Malevos tries to atone for the pain he caused in the past

Plotline #11: Lord Stenner of Bair determines to free his sister from bondage no matter what it costs him.

Plotline #12: Winder, a Kladdan servant, wants only to go home to Kladdis

Plotline #13: Queen Amalia falls in love with the one man she can never have, the outlaw Daigard

Once you have the main plot and the subplots identified, show how the different subplots might affect the main plot, and how they could make it harder for the main character to achieve his/her story goal. What structure (Linear or Interwoven) would be best for each subplot, and why? Is there one subplot you might leave open to lead into a possible sequel or series? Which one and why?

Take **25 minutes** to finish this exercise. Set your timer and start writing now.

Examples From My Class Writing

THESE ARE EXAMPLES OF WRITINGS I do in my workshops along with my students as I teach each lesson. Please bear in mind that they are done in the 15-30 minute sessions and have not been edited or corrected.

Lesson #1: From Situation to Subplot
Situation: Engaged Couple Scene

"Okay," the best man, Brad said, standing and raising his champagne flute, "let's toast the happy couple!"

The whole room cheered and lifted their glasses.

Magda forced herself to smile, first at Brad, then at Jenna and Aaron at the head of the table. A warm glow radiated from both of them, enhanced by the candles alight in the room.

Happy, indeed, Magda thought. *The proverbial match made in heaven. Or is it hell?*

"Aren't they cute?' Sheilah, already half drunk, leaned toward Magda. "I just love happy endings, don't you? The bitch and the bastard, together forever."

"Yeah, you're a real romantic," Cary snarled, yanking his wife upright. "Drunk, sloppy and romantic. As usual."

"Oh, fuck you." Sheilah waved a dismissive hand and giggled. She drained her glass, then waved it in the air for a passing waiter to refill.

Magda rose, walked over to the bank of windows and looked out at the sideways-blowing snow. Her palms itched and she had trouble breathing. Soon, now, things would change. Would the lack of electricity cause them problems? Would it all go according to plan? She turned and looked at Sheilah, who sat weaving in her chair. She'd gotten so drunk so fast. If she passed out, all their plans would be for naught.

She took a step toward the table and stopped when Brad stood. He spoke to Cary, then lifted Sheilah to her feet and began guiding her toward the window.

"'Smatta with you?" she asked, as she hiccupped her way across the floor. "I'm fine, don' need no air. Jes a little more hair of the dog, y'know."

"You've had too much hair already, Sheilah," Brad said, his eyes locked on Magda. She nodded and opened her clutch.

"Ain't 'nuff hair to stuff those two down my throat." Sheilah tried to pull away from Brad, but he tightened his hands on her shoulders. "Lookit them up there, like they own the world. Hate 'em, I really do."

"Sheilah," Magda said as she slipped the revolver to Brad. "It's a party. Don't—"

"Don't what? Spoil their special day?" Sheilah's voice rose; heads turned their way. Aaron started to rise. "What about me? What they did to me? They ruined my life, they did. Why shouldn't everyone know it, know what they are?"

Brad slapped the gun into Sheilah's hand and whispered in her ear.

"Show them, Sheilah. Show them how you really feel."

"Wha'?" Sheilah said as Brad, half-hidden behind Sheilah, lifted her hand, his finger on hers as together they squeezed the trigger.

"No! Sheilah, don't!" Magda screamed.

Aaron collapsed, red blooming on his pristine white shirt. People screamed and ran toward Aaron or the door, or dove beneath the tables. Brad knocked the gun from Sheilah's grasp and yanked her arms behind her back.

"Aaron!" Jenna shouted, "Aaron! She shot him, my God, he's dead! He's dead!"

Magda turned her back to the room and smiled at Brad. Mission accomplished.

Main Plot Possibility:

Magda and Brad are freelance assassins who work together. They have only one condition: they will not war on women or children. All their 'hits' must have eluded justice and need to be killed to stop them. Her cover: she's a very successful ad executive who travels the world for her clients. His cover: he owns a highly successful insurance investment firm which necessitates him traveling the world for business. They have been hired by the CIA to rid San Francisco of a major drug cartel leader, who, unknown to them, has discovered their identities and is making plans to eliminate them on a permanent basis.

Possible subplots:

1. The Aaron/Jenna plot: Aaron secretly runs a white sex slave ring and Magda's cousin's daughter was caught in it. This is personal revenge for them. Reveals their principles and humanity.

2. Brad's brother is a special agent for the FBI and runs a task force charged with bringing down the Ghostly Duo as they are known in law enforcement circles. This shows the dilemma of good vs evil, or evil done for good's sake.

3. Magda is pregnant with Brad's child and doesn't want him to know because he is married. But she wants to keep the baby and get out of the business, but she doesn't want to leave Brad to work alone.

4. Brad's wife suffers from MS and has begun to deteriorate and Brad wants to spend more time with her. But he doesn't want Magda to have to work alone.

5. Brad is having a crisis of conscience. He had at one time wanted to become a priest and the urge has returned even more strongly. But how can a professional killer stop killing those that need it and devote himself to pacifism and God?

Exercise #2: From the Past to Subplot
Main Plot Scene: In the Airport

"Put that away!" Jarrod hissed, shoving my hand down. "Are you crazy? What if someone sees it?"

"If Elsan finds us, you'll be glad I have it."

I glared at Jarrod and tucked the disintegrator into my front pocket where I could reach it easily if need be. Jarrod glanced around at our fellow travelers, none of whom appeared the slightest bit interested in us. Eslan was nowhere in sight. Which did not mean he wasn't around somewhere, watching.

"And how do you expect to get it on the plane?" Jarrod growled into my ear. I smiled up at him and batted my lashes.

"Using my charm and good looks, of course," I said, knowing I'd merely <u>dazzle whoever searched</u> me on the on-ramp. Sometimes it actually helped to be a sorceress.

Jarrod shook his head and turned away from me. He stood, his proud profile limned by the dual suns, as he stared out the ocular at the hovering shuttles that loaded and disgorged their passengers.

"We'll never get away, Oraya," he murmured, more to himself than me, I think. "Elsan will hunt us to the ends of the universe."

"Maybe. But it might be the time—"

A thunderous rumble cut my words short. Jarrod spun and shoved me behind him, heroic jerk that he was. I had the gun in my hand before he pushed me down and crouched himself, using the bank of upholstered seats as cover. The noise grew louder, erupted into flash-bangs that had people running amok, screaming, scattering belongings in their errant paths. Large chunks of ceiling rained down, felling fleeing passengers and airline personnel. Outside the window, a bright flash bleached the color from the scene as a shuttle erupted into pieces. I shoved the disintegrator into Jarrod's hand and scrabbled in my carry-on bag.

"Eslan?" I asked, but Jarrod shook his head.

"Too messy, even for him. It must be <u>a terrorist faction</u>." He powered up the weapon, his orchid eyes glinting a mix of anger and excitement. "Just our luck to be caught in an attack."

I spilled out the caragel and mare's foot, built a small pyramid of clover as well, and waved the wemben withe at the four elemental corners while I chanted just as a nearby explosion brought half the outer wall down beside us. Thank the goddess, the enchantment held. For a few minutes at least, nothing could penetrate our bubble of protection.

Main Plot:

Oraya and Jarrod, sorceress and sorcerer, must fulfill a 1,000 yr old prophecy in order to save mankind from extinction. They must find <u>the long-lost Pentad</u>, a mythical 5-sided chalice that <u>arcane lore claims</u> will bring the 5 warring planets into perfect harmony, restore balance and end the coming destruction of humanity. They are sought by the evil Coalition government, headed by Eslan, who will do anything and kill anyone to retain power over the warring factions.

Character Bios:

Jarrod is 37, newly come to his sorcerer powers, which he still distrusts. Three years ago <u>he lost his wife and three children</u> when Eslan, forewarned of Jarrod's still-buried powers, blew up his house. Unfortunately for Eslan, Jarrod was not home at the time, though his family was. His action triggered <u>Jarrod's powers</u> and spurred him to develop them and take revenge on Eslan. Jarrod had worked as <u>a medical aid in a forensic hospital,</u> where wizards and scientists from all 5 planets worked together to end the plagues that had been sweeping through the coalition for decades. Once addicted to <u>holo-horse riding and racing</u>, he now thinks of nothing except wreaking vengeance on Eslan and his murder squad.

Oraya, twenty-nine, is a born sorceress, heir apparent to the <u>Shanto Church of Unification</u>, and one of the most powerful witches of the movement. She was sent to train Jarrod and turn him from his path of vengeance into helping restore full harmony before mankind becomes extinct. Her powers are second nature to her and she relies on them almost to the exclusion of technology. But she is also very smart, and knows when to <u>accept technical aid</u> when necessary. She <u>lives her life according to</u>

natural law as dictated by the goddess, and accepts her destiny to ascend the Throne of Purity and head the church. She had been working with Jarrod for a year and a half, but is having little luck in turning him from the path of destruction, or getting him to understand the Unification's cause, which is why they keep running afoul of Eslan and his troops.

Possible Subplots:

1. Oraya's attraction to Jarrod grows as she learns more and more about him. But to remain pure for her destiny as the head of the church, she must deny the mounting love she feels for Jarrod.

2. Natural law is being subverted by the Coalition and the warring terrorist factions, and often natural laws don't hold true anymore. This causes Oray to begin to doubt herself and her destiny.

3. Jarrod stubbornly refuses to understand the true meaning of their mission, and as a result sabotages it from carelessness. The reason behind his refusal to comprehend is that he is attracted to Oraya and feels disloyal to his dead wife and children.

4. Jarrod's training in the forensic hospital gives him an advantage over Oraya and allows him to subvert her training.

5. The terrorist factions all want to capture Oraya and Jarrod and turn them to work for their goals, not the good of humanity.

6. The Pentad is not lost, but is being protected by the Shanto church hierarchy. They do not want Oraya to find it, and misdirect her with false premonitions and pronouncements.

7. Jarrod gets caught up in a holo-racing scam that opens him to blackmail and that threatens to destroy the progress he and Oraya have made in finding the Pentad.

8. They locate the Pentad and discover that it cannot do any of the things rumor has claimed it can, that the prophesy was falsified. They are left having to save humanity through their own efforts.

Exercise #3: From the Present to Subplot

Life Area Subplots:

Bio #1: Nellie Frobisher, 94, a social activist dynamo, always roots and works for the underdog no matter who that is, human or not. She married her HS sweetheart just before he went off to WWII, where he died on the beaches of France, leaving her pregnant with twins. She had a boy and a girl who she ruled with an iron fist, terrified they would up and leave her, too. Which, of course, they did once they went to college. They never came back to Ruckshaw, though out of duty they call her once a month or so. Nellie became head librarian, first for the school system, then for the town public library, and sits on the Town Council and is responsible for keeping any kind of true development out of the town. She is stubborn, irascible and demanding. Everyone in town is terrified of her. This is her town and no one is going to mess with it.

Bio #2: Anton Aronsky, 35, an architect and developer who moved to town because his wife, who he met in college, wanted to be near her family (Kara Leigh is from Ruckshaw) once their kids started coming along. He has been traveling in order to work, but wants to stay home with his family more, and so is quietly buying up the turtle land so he can build a housing development that will connect the two sides of the town and bring some prosperity to the area. He is well aware of the status of the turtles and has built in accommodation for them, but, led by Nellie, most town's people don't understand that. He has lined up investors for the project who are about to pull out because of the delays. He's also an avid fisherman and hunter, often spending his weekends on the river that runs through the turtle's land or in the surrounding forests hunting elk, deer and bear.

Bio #3: Bristol Barton, 42, a con man who has come to Ruckshaw to hide from the police who are looking for him after his last caper. He grew up as part of the circus and learned how to pick pockets and razzle-dazzle people out of their money at a young age. He is glib, a social talker, who puts on many faces depending on who he is with. He has obtained a job at the local bank—with forged references—and has his eye on embezzling the investment funds Anton Aronsky has deposited for his development. It was at the deposit window that he met Misty Crowler, who teaches kindergarten. For the past six months he has been using her as a colorful cover, wooing her in public to legitimize his presence even further. Not until he saw her talking to Anton Aronsky did he realize that he truly loves her, and doesn't want to lose her when he finally achieves his goal of taking the money.

Subplots:

Nellie: Subplot = Private: her children fear she is starting to fail mentally (in truth they are simply tired of her tirades) and believe it's time for her to stop working, move away from Ruckshaw and retire to an assisted living home near one of them. They also believe they should have power of attorney to handle her money, which they believe she spreads around indiscriminately.

Anton: Subplot = Interpersonal: Anton needs to get people to understand that he will be saving the turtle's nesting grounds, and needs to try to get people to listen to him, which Nellie keeps undermining. He concocts a strategy to wine and dine the movers and shakers of the town in his own home, to make them "friends" so they will be more amenable to listening to his theories about how to divide up the land, instead of simply going along with whatever Nellie demands.

Anton: Subplot = Personal: Anton's wife, Kara Leigh, sides with Miss Nellie and doesn't want the land developed. She tries to get Anton to abandon the project and he keeps trying to get her to understand his vision. They argue more and more and grow apart; eventually he begins to suspect she is having an affair and he is about to lose her if he continues forging ahead with the project that will keep them in the town. But if he leaves, will she and the children go with him?

Bristol: Subplot = Professional: The assistant manager at the bank has never liked Bristol, and when he is up for a promotion she decides to try to bring him down. She starts researching his references, which were never fully vetted, just accepted as valid, and discovers discrepancies such as: the real Bristol Barton died twenty years before at age 12. Bristol must try to find a way to discredit her findings while maintaining a professional presence in the bank.

Bristol: Subplot = Personal: His relationship with Misty Crowler, as he falls more deeply in love with her, he must decide how much of who he truly is to reveal to her, and decide whether he wants to continue to pursue the money and leave town or settle down, marry and become the boring old family man he has always feared he would eventually be. Love or money, that is his choice.

New Main Plot:

Choice = **Bristol Personal Subplot:** The assistant manager at the bank has never liked Bristol, and when he is up for a promotion she decides to try to bring him down. She starts researching his references, which were never fully vetted, just accepted as valid, and discovers discrepancies such as: the real Bristol Barton died twenty years before at age 12. Bristol must try to find a way to discredit her findings while maintaining a professional presence in the bank.

Possible Subplots:

1. His relationship with Misty Crowler, who he has fallen in love with. Does he reveal who he is or not?

2. His need for money exacerbated by the fact that the last person he stole from finds him and threatens to harm him—or Misty—if he doesn't pay him back, as opposed to calling the cops. This person is a crook in his own right and has no qualms about hurting or killing anyone who gets in his way.

3. The bank manager falls in love with Barton and uses the discrepancies in his references to blackmail him into a relationship.

4. Barton gets involved with the turtle issue as a way to ingratiate himself into the town, and pull the wool over Anton's eyes, and runs afoul of Nellie.

5. Barton's circus family finds him and tries to blackmail him into letting them in on his scheme, which he has decided to abandon. They threaten to tell Misty who they all are, and who and what Barton is, if he doesn't cooperate.

6. The FBI agent who has been on Barton's trail discovers him in Ruckshaw, but sees how he has changed and is helping the townsfolk settle the turtle issue. Now he must decide whether or to haul him in or let him go.

7. Nellie gets to know Barton and decides to trust him—as usual for her, on a whim—and gives him power of attorney over her money,

which is substantial because she invested in the town over the years and is one of the largest landlords in the county. Now Barton must decide if he will be honest with her money, or steal it.

8. Barton, at Misty's urging, starts going to church with her and finds the Lord. He confesses to the priest all his past misdeeds and what his plans are concerning the development funds and Nellie's money, and now must struggle to decide whether or not to continue with his nefarious deeds or follow his new-found spiritual morals.

9. The priest who hears Barton's confession must struggle with the secret he holds, while trying to counsel Barton and Misty about marriage, which he doesn't believe should occur.

10. Barton has an affair with Kara Leigh, Anton's wife, as a way to keep Anton off-kilter until he can steal the funds.

Lesson #4: From the Future to Subplot

This is an exercise that explores a story on which I am working:

Character: Aviva Jellinski, 32, homicide detective; Story goal: to solve the murders of people who bear a striking resemblance to her.

Daily Goals: Stay on top of paperwork; take clothes to the cleaners; to not drink more than 6 cups of coffee

Short-Term Goals: Take the Lieutenant's exam; learn to cook French cuisine; re-qualify at the shooting range; investigate psychic phenomena to see why she's so connected to crime scenes

Long-term Goals: Marry Steece Hayes and settle down and have two children; purchase a house to get out of apartment living; transfer to the FBI and become a profiler

Daily Possible Subplot: Aviva never has time to get to the cleaner's and she keeps running out of clothes. She is gaining a rep as a clothes horse, which makes her lash out angrily (she feels disrespected) and causes problems with other officers, who put roadblocks in her way when she's investigating the crime by losing paperwork, not giving her messages, etc.

Short-Term Possible Subplot: Investigating psychic phenomena can cause her to start doubting herself and what she feels and senses so she dismisses vital clues. It can also cause her fellow officers to make fun of her and the Captain and Chief to begin doubting her ability to do the job. The more she learns, the more she fears who and what she is.

Long-term Possible Subplot: Aviva loves Steece Hayes, and wants to marry him and have kids (her clock is ticking), without giving up her job. But when he's around he ridicules her belief in parapsychology and laughs at her fears about the things she experiences, and he puts down as 'coincidence' the way the victims look like her. Basically he wants her to quit her job and either stay home, or do something 'normal,' like secretarial work. They start to fight and she comes in to work frazzled and upset, which causes her to either miss clues and snap at witnesses and other officers, or be harsh and inflexible.

Secondary Character: Captain Hosea Danville, 53; story goal: to run his department so well he becomes chief of police.

Daily goals: keep his officers in line; dress for the position he wants; fend off pressure from 'upstairs'; to ignore the pains he feels in his chest.

Short-term Goals: Learn to play golf; learn to like, or at least understand, opera; get rid of the dead wood in the department; keep his mistress a secret

Long-term Goals: Become chief of police; divorce his wife and marry his mistress; retire to a condo on the water in Florida; increase his investments by whatever means necessary

Daily Possible Subplot: Danville needs to keep his heart condition secret or he'll be forced to retire early, but the strange murders and Jellinski's apparent connection to them is causing problems. He tries to get her taken off the cases, but the Chief puts her back on. Then she starts in about psychic crap and his heart really kicks up.

Short Term Possible Subplot: He takes golf lessons so he can play with the movers and shakers as he moves up the ladder, which puts him between the street cops and detectives, and the upper echelon who want fast results. He has to keep pressuring Aviva and the others for results that he knows aren't going to be found that fast.

Long-Term Possible Subplot: Danville's wife discovers he has a mistress and she comes into the station and causes trouble for him. It gets physical on her part and that gets the other cops involved and he has to decide whether or not to press charges. But she is a friend of Aviva's, which causes problems when he gives Aviva orders about the case.

Subplots With the Most Complications:

1. Aviva and Steece subplot will complicate the main plot by taking Aviva's concentration away from the murders she is investigating, and by making her question herself and her abilities. What is she willing to give up for love? Or is her job just too important to her to include a normal married life?

2. Danville's heart condition will complicate the main plot because Danville refuses to acknowledge he has problems. He blames Aviva when his heart acts up and works to undermine her so she can be taken

off the cases and eventually drilled out of the station, either let go or transferred. He refuses to allow her the room she needs to properly investigate the crimes, so she'll fail and he doesn't have to deal with his heart anymore.

Lesson #5: Subplot Sparkers

This details the first three of the seven Subplot Sparkers possibilities for my Aviva story:

1. **Who Else Has an Agenda? a. Steece Hayes** is connected with a government group that studies paranormal abilities. He was sent to study Aviva and then to convince her to come with him to their hidden lab for testing. Complication: Aviva falls in love with him, but becomes suspicious of his emotions, so she starts holding him at arm's length and he has to figure out how to let her know who he is before his superiors step in and simply have her abducted.

b. Also, Baxter Brighton, the psychologist treating drug addict/prostitute Venice Warbley, suspects she is a multiple personality, and has visions of studying her and producing the definitive book on the phenomenon based on his work with her, not really caring if she integrates successfully or not. In fact, he feels it's better if she doesn't, because that will give him more time with each personality, more fodder for his book, and more prestige with his peers.

2. **Main Plot Ripples:** Aviva tries to track down information on the first woman who is killed. She tracks the purchase of shoes and a skirt from a receipt from a second-hand shot. She goes in and interviews the man working in the store, Paul Maitland, who becomes attracted to

Aviva. He keeps calling and asking her out, running into her in odd places (on purpose), and disturbs her feelings for Steece, making her doubts loom larger than they normally would. And that tug between Steece and Paul distracts her from the case.

3. **Hero's Vulnerabilities: a. Aviva hates cell phones**, certain she will get brain cancer if she keeps using one, which is necessary for her work. She has an old, outdated flip phone and won't bring it near her head when using it, so she has trouble hearing and being heard. And she keeps turning hers off, and so misses important calls, then doesn't remember how to access her voice mail and has to keep asking one of her detectives how to do it. Biggest miss: a call from the killer.

b. **Also, she is a clothes horse**, loves new outfits, is always sending away for things from catalogues (no time to go shopping in person). She spends way more than she should and is always short of money when rent and utilities are due. She also gets a rep as a clothes horse, which destroys a lot of her credibility with her squad and especially the Captain and the upper echelon in the force.

c. **She has blackouts** she can't understand and is afraid to talk about. As they grow longer and more debilitating, they begin to interfere with both her personal and professional life.

Lesson #6, 7, 8 and 9: Examples are given in the lessons themselves, and I don't do #9, since I wrote the book and know which are main and which are subplots. If you're having problems with these lessons, drop me a line and I'll do what I can to help.

Afterword

"Always grab the reader by the throat in the first paragraph, sink your thumbs into his windpipe in the second, and hold him against the wall until the tag line."

~Paul O'Neil

BEING A WRITER IS a fascinating occupation. By its very nature it forces us to dig deeply into our inner core, face those things that frighten us, are painful or perhaps even disgust us. And then we bring those things into the light of day—on a piece of paper, whether physical or virtual—and transform them into a story that entertains, teaches and/or enlightens whoever reads it. In our own way, writers help make the world a better place.

The amount of skill needed to do all that successfully is known fully only to those engaged in the practice itself. Readers come in two main groups: those who cannot conceive of what it takes to write a story, much less an entire book; and those who think it's easy to sit down and pound out a story or book in, they think, a few days or weeks. But only the brave actually attempt it.

Everything we learn to increase our writing skills helps improve us as human beings. We learn how to see, to hear, to contemplate and to understand in ways that most others never do. We learn to find the weaknesses in our heroes and to use them to strengthen their characters. And, in a way, we are also strengthened. We search for the good in our villains and use that to make them human and comprehensible. And in facing our own dark side, we understand more about ourselves and those around us.

In this *Workbook #5*, you have explored two of the essential skills you need to craft compelling, unforgettable stories, whether they are pure fiction or arise from your own life as memoirs—how to infuse your stories with **conflict and tension** that keeps readers turning pages, and how to use **subplots** to add dimension and depth to your tales. But these are only two of the skills you need to find your strength as a writer. The other workbooks in the *Write It Right* series will give you exactly what you need to become the best writer you can possibly be, with exercises that can be used over and over again as your skills continue to grow and develop. If you haven't yet acquired any of the other workbooks in the series, here's a short recap of what you can expect:

Workbook #1: Character, Setting, Story consists of the first three units of the *Write It Right* series: Character, setting and story are the first three essential elements of story telling, the foundation blocks, so to speak, for without compelling characters in unforgettable settings acting out amazing stories, there is nothing to write about. In this workbook you will find 9 lessons and exercises on creating compelling characters, 7 exercises on crafting unforgettable settings and 10 exercises on where to find ideas and how to analyze them for story potential. Twenty-six lessons/exercises in one volume.

Workbook #2: Point of View (POV) will take you through the murky waters of point of view (POV). In these 15 lessons and exercises you will learn about straight, emotional and classic POV types, and the advantages and disadvantages of each one. You will then experience their variations and understand when to use which POV type to best advantage in your story telling.

Workbook #3: Plot, Dialogue continues your journey along the writer's path with 8 exercises on crafting flawless, intricate plots that sizzle off the page. You'll discover what plot actually is, the importance of a through line, how to analyze ideas for viable plots and where to find plots in the world around you. The Unit on dialogue presents 8 lessons that will show you how to write sparkling dialogue that sounds perfectly natural while still addressing the six necessary ingredients that make dialogue an integral part of the story. You will learn how to write for your audience, make your characters' voices unique, use idioms to infuse verisimilitude, how to tag properly and how to incorporate subtext into what your characters say.

Workbook #4: Scenes, Style/Voice contains lessons and exercises that will help you understand the 9 different types of scene structures and how each affects the rhythm and pacing of your stories. The Unit on Style/Voice will help you develop your own unique writing style, a clear, consistent voice that will stand out among all the others and be readily recognizable as yours alone.

Workbook #6: Brilliant Beginnings, Extraordinary Endings gives you 8 different formats for opening your stories and 8 unique ways of ending your stories. In Brilliant Beginnings you will also learn how to polish that all-important first sentence/first paragraph/first page so that readers are compelled to continue reading. And in Extraordinary

Endings, you will learn the secrets to choosing the proper ending for whatever story you write, so that readers smile and say, "I'm so glad I read that!"

Look for the entire *Write It Right: Exercises to Unlock the Writer in Everyone* workbook series on Amazon.com in print format. Each individual unit is also available in digital format in the Kindle store, but the workbooks themselves are available only in print because I feel that is the most useful format for serious writers. You can have the book open on your desk as you work on the exercises either by hand of on the computer, and not have to keep switching from one window to another to check on the exercise parameters or re-read the lesson as you work.

Thank you for purchasing this Workbook. I hope you find it helpful on your writing journey. If you do, please take the time to write a review on Amazon.com, since that's where most of my sales come from. In this digital age of social media, it's reader reviews that best help sell books. As does word of mouth, so be sure to tell all your writer friends about the Write It Right series, so they can also benefit from the program.

Also, if you'd like, please drop by my website (www.SusanTuttleWrites.com) and leave a comment or two about the photos and story/character/setting ideas you'll find (Category: Woman of 1,000 Words), the weekly writing prompts that post every Wednesday (Category: Write Over The Hump), about the *Write It Right* program, or any other writing subject that comes to mind. Or email me at aim2write@yahoo.com. I'd love to hear from you.

Susan's Books

I NEVER THOUGHT, WHEN I started to write my own stories, that one day I would produce an entire series of workbooks on how to write fiction (and creative nonfiction, because these days that genre needs to be structured in the same manner as fiction). I never thought it even when I started teaching fiction writing. Getting my novels out was my main goal. But life has a way of guiding you down paths you don't even know are there, and this is where I've been led.

What follows is a listing of the books I have out in either print or ebook format, or both—and those in process of being readied for print/e-format. The *Write It Right Workbooks* head the list, but I'm also adding in my fiction titles at the end (suspense and paranormal suspense) in case you might like to take a peek at them, too (all available on Amazon.com and Amazon Kindle). I think they're pretty great, but then, as the author, I'll admit I'm a bit prejudiced. (Okay, lots prejudiced!)

My hope is that my *Write It Right Workbooks* will help unlock the talent and amazing stories that reside in each and every one of you. Happy writing!

Susan's Nonfiction Books

Write It Right Workbooks available from Amazon Print:

Workbook #1: Units 1, 2, 3: Character, Setting, Story

Workbook #2: Unit 4: POV,

Workbook #3: Units 5, 6: Plot, Dialogue

Workbook #4: Units 7, 8: Scenes, Style/Voice, Conflict

Workbook #5: Units 9, 10: Conflict/Tension, Subplot

Workbook #6: Units 11, 12: Beginnings, Endings*

E-versions available from Amazon on Kindle:

Workbook #1: Character

Workbook #2: Setting

Workbook #3: Story

Compendium #1: Character, Setting, Story

*Coming Fall/Winter 2015

Susan's Fiction Books

Suspense
> *Tangled Webs*
> *Sins of the Past*
> *Piece By Piece*

Paranormal Suspense
> *Proof of Identity*

Waiting for Covers:
> **A Matter of Identity**, historical suspense
> **Death in the Valley** (3 award-winning short stories in one volume)

Works in Progress:
> *Obsession,* a novel of suspense
> *Stealing Shyon*, an adult fantasy
> The Skylark Series: paranormal detectives
>> *Murder Under the Oaks* (short story in SinC anthology)
>> *The Somewhen Murder* (novella from short story)
>> *Dead Ringer* (novella from short story)
>> *Someone Else's Eyes*
> **Destany's Daughter,** a paranormal YA / Adult fantasy series

Look for my suspense novels coming soon as audio books on Audible, Amazon and iTunes.